Daniel Evan Weiss is the author of the novels *The Roaches Have No King*, *Hell on Wheels*, and *The Swine's Wedding*, all published by Serpent's Tail. He lives in New York City.

Author's note:

I have taken loving license with the great borough of Brooklyn.

Honk
if you love Aphrodite

Daniel Evan Weiss

FOR DELILAH

Library of Congress Catalog Card Number: 98-89856

A catalogue record for this book is available from
the British Library on request

First published in 1999 by Serpent's Tail,
4 Blackstock Mews, London N4

Website: www.serpentstail.com

Typeset in 11pt Bembo by Avon Dataset Ltd, Bidford on Avon, B50 4JH

Printed in Great Britain by Mackays of Chatham plc

10 9 8 7 6 5 4 3 2 1

Garden of the insipid delights

A great opossum of a man, body-hair long and spiky,
flesh of dough, crawls naked across a spattered stage.
Riding a saddle girded round his giving middle sits
a woman in an obsidian suit.

She reins his head by a bit soft against his mouth;
she rains obloquy on him, though generic and toothless;
she rains blows on his buttocks, but too gentle to cut.
She reigns over him! he repeats.
As he fawns she yawns.
It is I who feel true pain.

Beside them rises a cross, man attached. He must know torment.
No, he is neither nailed nor hanging;
his feet rest sure on a step;
his hands are free as the insects circling his aging G-string.
His nipples are gently tented by piercing rings;
the woman pulling looks away, so gruesome
is the spectacle.

She hoods him in black leather and zips closed his face,
muffling endless thanks to her, his mistress;
it is relief for her and me both.
She lights a cigarette, compresses her cuticles.

Throughout Club Hades mortals seek pleasure through pain;
yet they cannot abandon themselves to it:
every cheek is rouged by false lashes, every scream
a performance. There is no note of passion here.

When was the Fall of love? Why was I brought
to witness? The tedium smarts worse than quirt.
Though not the fiery Tartarus deep in the bowels
of Mother Earth, there never was a truer hell
than this.

A tip of a whip does not snap, but rather
thumps the podium. An announcement: a contest!
Judges sweep the floor; revelers' votes will name
the victor. I cannot muffle my mirth as I await
the tally.

The chief arbiter calls, "We have a winner. The cutest guy here
is the slave of the ugliest one. He's really cute, too."

I look about to a circle of fingertips. Alas, it is I
who have been chosen. I am most magnificent
of males; and Father is most grotesque, he who is fastening
firm golden cuffs about my fine wrists. Would
men and women cheer if they knew we alone
in this shallow hell are no act?

All commend Father's hideousness, which they ascribe
to costume; if only it could be removed. Enraged,
he bolts me with matchless strength. I know better
than to beg forbearance. Once done, he laughs so hard
as to fissure the char of his face; but beneath it
lies only more char.

The crowd applauds our drama; it provides
what escapes them: passion.

There is but one who can rescue me – the one
who enticed me here and abandoned me.

Aphrodite. Mother.

Aphrodite's snare

All Aphrodite's sons claim the golden goddess' same power
to create love and destroy it, to transfigure lives
by attuning hearts. Theirs is delusion. I have suffered
endless tellings of many wondrous trips to the mortal world,
to conclude my brothers share the swat of a nosegay.

I alone of Aphrodite's issue am flawless of form. Always
I supposed my amorous powers would exceed theirs
by the same magnitude as does my beauty.
Unlike them, I had never been sent by her
to the brown earth; the most modest mortal coupling
had never been entrusted me. I had been held back,
a jewel in safekeeping.

Immortal females flew to my bed like milkweed to dark felt.
I understood the lure was not to me alone but also
to my thickness with Aphrodite. I took no umbrage;
who would not want to warm by the golden goddess,
the greatest fire?

I drank her sight, her smell daily. Every mortal and immortal,
gorgeous to egregious, claims the right to dream
of lying with her. But I would be damned for thinking
I was more than son.
It is true – Aphrodite is Mother. Yet is she not Aphrodite
to me as well?

For eons these two relations warred across my sculpted chest:
family members do not romance each other; but
who drew this sanction, and for whom? Aphrodite is held
by no one's rules. At long last I concluded:
neither should be her son.

But what to do? I had no one to consult; those few
who attain Aphrodite's bed are evicted before
they choose; none would aid me in becoming nearmost her.

Easy is my rapport with Mother on every theme; but for this
I found no words. I longed for her to know my heart;
but I was more afraid of her all-powerful spurn.

Facing an eternity unanswered at last unnerved
me most. Did she feel there should be greater between us?
I knew her love as Mother. I knew from others love
in every other form. Should the two be one?

The goddess of love would never answer straight.
Still, I needed one consultation.
How could her favor be won?

Thus it began.

I arrived in Aphrodite's lair, ringed with low fires,
redolent of perfumed conquest, strewn with pelts. Always
I could jest with her whether god and mortal hides
were among them. But this time I could not.

Seated at her dressing table, she did not hear my arrival –
or pretended so. Her gown slipped from shoulders to elbows,
exposing an alabaster back carved like no other. She evinced

surprise when she turned to me; why then did she not
conceal her cleavage? She raised her perfect arms to affix
more flowers in a garland already full. Beside this,
Achilles' panoply was gossamer.

I was bold in averring my intention for us two.
She laughed and took me in her soft arms. She said,
"I need you here. You are my ground, my humility.
You match my beauty, and so can resist my beauty.
It touches me how weak you are today; tomorrow
your strength will return."

Her tone abased me.

She bid me sit. She said, *"I have often thought of sending you*
to the teeming earth, where my amorous burdens are great.
But should you fail, you would know anguish; as cause of it,
I would be hateful in your eyes. That I could not abide."

I said, *"How could I, who have tenanted your womb,*
fail a duty of love?"

She said, *"You need reach into hottest flame*
and never recoil."

I looked straight at her. Could the mortal earth
offer anything more burning?

She touched my shoulder with magical fingers. She said,
"Olympus was once pristine, until mortal numbers mounted,
and their settlements crept like lizards up our slopes.
Every godly nose suffered their waste, every ear their din.
Motor miasma corroded the magnificent temples

built for us millennia earlier. We abandoned Olympus for
a purer, gentler mount.

"Our ancient Olympian lungs and knees were unequal
to struggle, so we did not arrogate territory. Instead,
deathless Demeter, in caterer's disguise, induced chefs
of golf-course-girted hotels, where argyled populations vacationed,
to distill a poisonous red root, camouflage it with rancid cream,
and call it a delicacy: borscht. Psyche induced men
– comedians – to demean publicly their own forebears.
Between food and humiliation, all mortals soon died
or were driven from Catskill. Only then did we secure it.

"Thus has been the toll on us all of this modern world,
beloved. Our tasks can no longer be achieved with
quick arrows through the heart. Should I have called on you?
Could you bear it?"

I said, *"I will succeed."*

Aphrodite, goddess of love, bowed her head; fire danced
in the gold of her hair. She said, *"No, I cannot risk you.*
Forgive a mother's selfishness."

I took her perfectly tapered hand. I said, *"Risk me. The reward*
will be great." She refused. I said, *"Then think of me.*
Who am I, but Aphrodite's perfect boy, languishing in Catskill,
a waste of beauty. I must be more."

For weeks she denied me. I pressed ever more passionate
entreaties upon her. At last she relented, perhaps more
from exhaustion than persuasion: I would be sent
to this messy earth to command mortal passion as she did.

I would prove worthy of the perch beside her
at the Catskill Council. Most, I would prove
deserving of her love.

Khoni Island

I offered Uncle Hermes a slim waist, that he might savor
my hair as he eased me skyward; instead he wrenched me
by my delicate wrist, disordering those same golden curls.
What else was this but envy of my crucial responsibility?

The mere messenger to the greater Olympians prattles
like a widow; this once I anticipated his words:
what was our destination, this Khoni? Yet this once
he did not speak. What sealed his rapid lips?

Uncle veered earthward, through a humid vein of gray.
Earth – where leathered men drive leathery beasts
to lever ploughs through rocky soil; where one olive's advent
is sufficient cause for universal inebriation. Khoni looked
no worthier of me than anywhere else.

I said, *"Talk, well-traveled Hermes! Talk now of Khoni
before I land."*

I turned to him. Uncle was gone! A flare overtook Helios
and his shining steeds in the western sky; it was he.
Disquietude clenched my vitals.

Like goose down I descended toward Khoni; fleet Hermes
had cast a spell over my eyes. Instead of rock and mud
in precarious perch over crashing shore, I saw constellations
as thick as the heavens yet brighter, in rapid motion,
of every hue of fermenting fish. The air was filled with

screams – but laughter too. To what chromatic hell
had Mother sentenced me?

A godly pinch on my own godly arm – the scene was real.
My first decision: what befitted the coming of a new Catskillian
upon the brown earth? Mother had not said. Perhaps
a fiery meteor thundering into the Khoni loam.
Mortals would race to my scorched crater, only
to see me rise, alive and impossibly gorgeous. No,
it would overwhelm.

Why not enter as Mother had? The long beach was quiet,
save for murmuring rolls of low tide. Upon one such beach,
eons past, Mother rose from foam girding
the great genitals of Uranus – those lonely organs
having been cleaved by his mischievous son Cronus.
This bloody act Mother redeemed: when she landed,
flowers grew in her steps. But where on Khoni would I find
a double of the mountainous member of primordial Uranus?

I neared the gray whitecaps. The sand was more
bawdy house floor than virginal bed, sown with food,
drink, and lust. I wondered if the goddess of love
could grow flowers here.

So too the waters were not what they seemed. Uncle Poseidon
beats white crests into baubles before their meek retreat
into the sea; these solid masses of foam washed out
just as they came in. My godly nose detected
a subversive element in the Khoni water, neither fish
nor fowl nor sea bottom decomposing. Nor was the color
any more Aegean blue than I am.

I was afraid to ride the fetid foam; would it dim my glow?

Unsweet my perfume? I devised a drier emulation
of Mother's entrance: I would do like her star and rise.

But how, in this sky? I thought to ask dark Hades
for a patch of humus to use as launch, but feared
the bargain he would drive. Then I heard a steel shriek
from far beneath my feet. A cleft in the Khoni ground
disgorged myriad mortals; it was there I began my climb.
My godly pith quickened. Surely I was first of the deathless
to debut on earth this way.

I know not what divine sinew I flexed as I ascended
the stairs – my grace is unconscious as a heartbeat –
but I tempered my godliness on the cusp of the underworld,
lest I offend the dark god. Still he chose to intrude.
Mother would punish a grab for my soul; he grabbed instead
for my soles – my sandals; one he tugged with pink tendrils
rising from a stair, the other with a flattened bag
savoring of insemination. He forced Helios behind
a celestial blot; any eclipse in thunder-loving Zeus' sky
is amply dire to loosen the entrails.

Sister Phobos, mistress of fear, spurred me up the stairs.
A collision sent me hurtling back towards Hades' realm.
Already I was caught. Where could I go if neither up nor
down? My shaken thoughts were long in clearing. It was
no celestial body dimming earth's light. It was a lone mortal:
a woman bent to adjust her footwear – a web of glowing colors
atop a black waffle. It was her skyward nates, her
prodigious pillows, and those alone, that obliterated the sun!
Feral Europeans long ago carved images of Mother
with colossal rears, but never the match of these.

From waist down the mortal wore a taut black cocoon;
when she uprose it conveyed so fully the turbulence
of the flesh within that a sailor the likes of
great Odysseus himself might have been warned off.

How could she attain such magnitude unless fatted
for sacrifice on this Khoni Island? In Catskill
even females of Mother's perfect proportion drape modestly –
yet here was full, brutal disclosure. I, Aphrodite's issue,
assumed I held all-embracing knowledge of gender ways.
Yet already I failed to gird female wiles on tiny Khoni.
And I was afraid.

When the woman departed, violet light filled the stairwell;
Helios had dipped over sky's edge. Atop the stairs
I surveyed the milling population. In appearance they were
to the beings of Catskill as are swollen ticks to thoroughbreds
whose blood they suck.

No matter: I had my mission among them. I let the throng
sweep me ahead. All about us were lights in every shape –
some bent into script, of colors even dawn-painting Aurora
did not know. Great roaring machines hurled wagons
of mortals through the air as if they too were deathless.
They cried for release – until safely earthbound, whereupon
they begged to be tormented by one more ride.

I walked webs of streets of booths of games of chance:
toss and land a coin upon a plate;
guess to the moment the final tilt of a spun wheel;
land a hoop on a form designed to rebuff it.
A messenger of love knows a certain uncertainty tantalizes;

but this? They could loose their lucre into a rushing river
and be as certain of its fate.

Last of the chanceless games pitted mortals against
leaden bottles so sturdy that Apollo himself
would be tested to drop them – yet contestants were allowed
but one toss of a ball from ten paces to hew all three.
Drawn by shelves of prizes, mortal after mortal
slapped down green currency and assumed the challenge.
Most throws struck nothing but the canvass behind.
Toppling the topmost bottle, just as total a failure,
allowed the proprietor to curse the contestants' luck
yet praise their skill – which was certain to improve.
And so players' pockets flattened.

One contestant wore a suit that glinted subtly
as a nymph's eyes. His shoes were cut from a calf
worthy of sacrifice to sky-ruling Zeus. Upon his shirt,
white as a tropical noon, hung a pendant of finest silk.

He held the ball against his lizard-pelt belt. He said, "Sandy
Koufax checks the sign from Johnny Roseboro. The bases are
filled with Yankees. The count is full, two down, bottom of the
ninth. One strike and the Dodgers win the Series. The crowd is
on their feet."

A fat man in similar finery said, "Throw the ball. The crowd
wants to sit down."

The first said, "Koufax cannot be rattled by the abuse of the
partisan Yankee Stadium crowd. He is too great."

The second said, "Throw the ball and we'll see how great you are."

The first said, "Wait. Mantle steps out of the box. He's toying with Koufax, trying to throw off his rhythm."

The second said, "Either that, or his knees are decomposing as he waits for the pitch."

The proprietor of the game said, "Anything wrong over here?"

The fat one said, "Just your everyday World Series pressure."

The thin one rocked back onto his rear leg; after looking suspiciously left and right, he brought forth his arm, releasing the ball with grimace and groan. If the bottles could be thought a corner column of a Grecian temple, the ball sailed high over what would be the column on the corner opposite.

The fat one said, "Ball four. Dodgers lose. Let's go."

A smaller mortal, dressed like these two, said, "Ball four? You mean ball twelve."

The thinner mortal laughed and presented more money. He said, "Sandy Koufax checks the sign from Johnny Roseboro. The bases are filled with Yankees. The count is full, two down, bottom of the ninth. One strike and the Dodgers win the Series. The crowd is on their feet."

The other two showered him with impatient abuse.
The thin mortal pointed to a great stuffed bear atop
the shelves of prizes. He said, "Babe Ruth called his home
runs. I'm calling that by the close of the evening, I will
present that to my wife."

So I first encountered the white shirt that would end
in my golden cuffs.

The great bear

A thousand questions I burn to ask Mother; if my arms
were not shackled I would commit them to paper.
Why does she not return so we can speak? Though
she judges my quest failed, she now sees my heart
to the core, and knows its purity. Why torment me?
Am I not due the courtesy accorded any sincere suitor?

That day in her perfumed lair, hides about, I asked Mother
to expound on the command of mortal passion. I wanted
to descend to earth equipped.

She said, *"You know love as the bee knows flowers;
the wisdom is inside your immortal heart."*

I said, *"But in which mortal flower, of the bushy billions,
shall I invest my pollen?"*

She said, *"The bee departs the hive without a map;
I depart Catskill the same."*

I begged a mite more. She said, *"Does sky-shaking Zeus
inquire who should feel his white-hot bolts? Or
gay Dionysus who shall twice taste his vintage,
influxing and egressing? You must prove yourself
not only by action, but also by judgement. I will not
tell you more, lest I burden and confuse you."*

Is there a greater burden than unbreakable chains?
Would it have confused me to have a paragraph more?

In Khoni I was already asea: though my interest
was raised by this mortal, I did not know quite why.
Far from beautiful, he was past an unprepossessing prime,
thin and scant of hair. Though he competed for his wife,
he was an incompetent archer, drawing dollars
from his pocket quiver, letting fly again and again
without success. Vigor he expended on his tosses;
yet he smiled at each failure; there was no heroic struggle.

He removed his elegant jacket, rolled his sleeves above
the elbow. Thus his new Koufax strategy. And now mine:
I decided I would aid him though I did not understand him;
there was no gain in delay. I guided the next throw
of Stanley (so his friends called him) with the speed
of fearless Ares' arrow; the bottles scattered like wrens.
Strangers cheered the rare success; the mouths
of Stanley's friends, flapping in derision, shut like
fishes' on flies.

Stanley short sleeves pointed to the bear on the top shelf,
the greatest of all prizes. The proprietor denied him.
He said, "For the big one you gotta do it twice, young fella."

Stanley short sleeves said, "Twice? You can't tell me now, after
I've been playing for half an hour. Where does it say that?"

The proprietor displaced the animal's leg; it carefully obscured
a faded "2" on the shelf edge.

Stanley's face reflected a contest of outrage and ambition.
The fat friend said, "Come on. Take a Winnie the Pooh and let's
get out of here. This guy's a crook."

Should I let him leave? Was the bear foremost
in his heart? Or were there more agonies for him to weigh?
My task on earth would not be so straight as I thought.
My decision: He would have what he claimed to want.
At length he reached once more into his wallet.

The fat friend said, "Christ. No wonder Koufax got arthritis."

My godly hand impelled this throw to invisible speed
before shattering the leaden bottles, perforating
the canvass behind them, splintering the booth back.
Shrapnel turned shelves of animals to tawny stuffing.
Mortals fled. The proprietor shoved the great bear,
miraculously untouched, at Stanley and begged him depart.

Awed were the aspects of the friends of Stanley short sleeves
as the three shambled toward the noise and lights
in Khoni center. An inflamed lover under Mother's spell
expends more time on a single stanza than I had
to secure him this goal – unaccountable though it was.
I prepared to depart the trash-pocked earth, triumphant.

I looked upon the heavens. Through brownish mist,
a marriage of Lord Poseidon's fog and mortal earth's
skyborne refuse, only great stars penetrate; Olympians
whose portraits depend on lesser lights cannot be discerned.
Most brilliant was Mother's – Venus, men call it;
too tame, too venereal a name to my ear. No matter.
Was this celestial smile not for me?

I needed to know Stanley short sleeves appreciated
the act consummated in her name; nothing rankles in Catskill
as does the mortal who thinks fortunes are formed
inside his grubby fists, like wet clay. Who makes
the clay, hands it to him, stiffens it when overworked,
softens it when overdried?

I intercepted Stanley. I said, "I salute you, master of the
parabolic trajectory, and your ursine spoils."

Bear-bearing Stanley and his friends looked upon me
like a beast bursting from wilds. The more inflated
friend spoke. He said, "Ah yes, a toga party. I remember them
well. I was young once. And devilishly handsome, believe it or
not."

The other friend seemed about to challenge this assertion,
but, lips quivering, contained his words. The prodigious one
laid a paw on my shoulder; the three walked on.

That he would touch me!
That Stanley would ignore me!

I stilled my godly rage: indeed I was errantly garbed
by local standards; there was nothing to pronounce my divinity.
In Khoni those dressed in garbage bags, or dining from them,
draw no more notice than those spreading over their faces
sugar spun into pink wool.

The three stopped at a grander, brighter booth; each squeezed
into a vehicle. At a bell's toll, the breath of life animated
the cars; but they sped in every direction. This was no race;
the object was rather to smash fellow riders.

My heart turned leaden with doubt. Was the conveyance
of the bear, ears aquiver with each impact, Stanley's
true desire? Or could his motive instead lie
in this rubber game? If so, how could the son
of the goddess of love help?
And should he?

The urine-stained earth had snared me with hubris:
showers of sparks rained from the ceiling where
cars' poles touched; they were false, fleeting lights, and
I had followed them.

A mother pulled her child past me, face blank and
streaked with gray, hair stringy and nameless brown.
The child's lips revealed a pink protrusion; it swelled to
half the volume of her unpleasant head. The mother
did not see; should I intervene? —
else the girl would surely die.

Other Khonis passed, indifferent. Could there be love
on the sputum-soaked planet when there was no compassion?
Then the report! The pink was gone; the girl, unaffected,
silently worked her jaw. I composed myself, or tried:
I feared this was one of countless horrors Mother chose
not to recount about the mortal earth.

If told all, still I would have come. What cause
had closed her ruby lips?

I now knew that for all my powers, I could not master,
certainly not soon, the vast vagaries of local life;
mortals do not wear their hearts exposed as immortals do,
anticipating instantaneous fulfillment of all desires.

How could I discharge my responsibility and breathe
air in Aphrodite's lair by Helios' next ride? Like
thunder-wielding Zeus I would employ the ultimate
earthly guile – I would imitate mortal flesh.
But unlike the godly father I did not aim for fleshly penetration.
I trained only for the heart.

To grow intimate with Stanley short sleeves
I would be his intimate – literally:
I would reproduce and dislocate
one of his disposable friends.

Becoming unbecoming Myron

Which friend? This was not a handsome choice. Lennie,
the smaller, rolled his lips over his words, as if
to retract them as soon as they were loosed.
I feared I could not maintain the tic, and would thus
betray my godliness.

Myron was ursine – bear seemed the night's theme.
Darkness was invented for his likes. Still, so ardent
was my desire to please Mother that I,
canon of deathless beauty, was happy to assume
his death-bound shape.

I followed the three to a food vendor, where
mortals ate standing, like cattle. They bought
small breads, slit lengthwise, inlaid with tepid bay tubes;
"hot dogs" better suits the defecation than the canines
from which they must issue. Myron the upholstered
ordered four; the others two.

Masticating Myron held one before his face.
Stanley short sleeves said, "Please don't leave anything
protruding. Not where people will associate you with me. And
don't get mustard on the bear."

Myron said, "You're worse than Minnie. Are there new
limitations on belching I should know about?"

Stanley short sleeves said, "As you well know, expulsion of gas is acceptable. But not of liquid or solids or any mixture thereof. Not on the Cyclone."

Lennie pursed lips said, "I don't want to go on that thing. My gastritis can't handle it any more."

Stanley short sleeves said, "If you've got gastritis, why are you piling onions and hot sauce on your dog? It's not your stomach that's giving out, my friend, it's your nerves."

Saliva-spitting Myron said, "I agree with Lennie. Let's not be held by precedent. Not after hours. Let's suffer on the ground."

Stanley with the rolled sleeves said, "Once a year we test our stomachs against the Cyclone. Otherwise where's the honor? Anybody can eat and stay on the ground."

So came to my godly ears this first mention of mortal honor.

Stanley short sleeves said, "If you want to make it easier on yourself, don't eat all four."

Myron the large said, "Hell with you, buddy. They're paid for."

The stout and pursed lipped ones lobbied to leave Khoni. Stanley said, "You guys are old."

Stung by the challenge, enormous Myron said, "I don't know how to take that, coming from a guy with a five dollar stuffed animal it cost fifty bucks to win. All right, let's go. We'll see who's old."

Thus was disclosed a third passion of Stanley short sleeves:
the Cyclone. It could not be that child of Poseidon,
the great wreathed storm that sucks countless mortals
to eternal sleep on the ocean floor; no one would choose that.

Stanley short sleeves said, "Look, you got mustard on the bear.
Was it too damn much to ask? I wanted to get it to Eileen
clean."

Myron of the gelatinous form said, "So wipe it off. It isn't the
Holy Grail. I'm smelling guilt for being out tonight."

Stanley said sharply, "I have nothing to feel the slightest bit
guilty about. Nothing."

Myron said, "Why don't you take your trophy home before
there's another catastrophe, like relish."

Stanley said, "I'll go home when I'm good and ready, thank
you."

Thus my first suggestion of conjugal love.

I followed lights hanging like dewdrops on overhead wires.
Then I saw it: the Cyclone – a towering steel track,
lit as was the Pharos of Alexandria, routing cars
over cliff-like drops and neck-cracking turns like chariots
drawn by maddened stallions over impossible trails.
Mortals volunteer – they pay – to be so racked;
they raise arms and cheer.

Why? There was terror in their visages – but also pleasure.
If one in a hundred – in a thousand – rides derailed,

how many would embark, how favorable the faces?
Now I look about Club Hades: if dominatrices plied
truly their trade, with switches that cut and brands that sear,
would any but the cobwebs be my company? It is safety
mortals love; simulated fear pleases because their lives
know no true excitement.

It was time to replace upholstered Myron. I struck him
with a parching thirst; hand on fat-ringed neck, he reeled
to a beverage stand. Lennie pursed lips said, "It's not gravity
between him and beer. It's that strong force, like the one that
holds the nucleus of the atom together."

Myron grasped beers with each hand, downing them
with a speed even veterans of his outrages found indecent.
Bladder soon bleating, Myron sought relief.
All was ready.

Immortals assume mortal forms: wise Athena becomes Mentor
– simple, instantaneous. So I expected to become
Myron the stout. I commanded my perfect body: Refashion!
But my beauty refused to surrender itself. It would have to be
subdued part by part. But how? Which muscles,
which nerves, would distend my abdomen from its
timeless rippled flatness? I felt a criminal; brilliant Socrates
drew no Olympian tears on his demise, so much
did his slovenly girth offend.

My breaths turned to pulsations. I burrowed to a site
deep within – I still know not where – and drummed at it
with every exhalation. I felt the strain of muscle,
the pain of muscle, the agony of muscle, and then – *snap!*
like a tree giving way after a night against a gale,

my immortal flesh surged forth. Back bent, shoulders bowed;
lapidary nates flattened like dough hitting rock.

Reflections in innumberable Khoni mirrors shattered my pride:
my unmatched face bloated and smeared; luxuriant hair,
save for a lunatic fringe, gone. I was a wreck
I wished immediately to abandon; but I had only
to scan the crowd to see how well I now fit.

The keystone to Myron's garb (which appeared about me)
was a lacerating belt; should it give way, my mass
would cascade toward the spittle-spotted asphalt.
When I reached to check the buckle, my arms
were engulfed in flesh. I could see neither waist
nor anything below. I would not fumble, lest I look
to be relieving myself. I did not yet know
mortals often do just that with no one heeding.

Again I would approach my charge, this time
as mortal Myron. What would be my first words?
An apology for my beer lust? No, Myron did not apologize.
Nor had I tested my voice, crucial though it was
to my disguise. I turned to talk to the air – I was one
of many in the teeming plaza doing so – only to witness
catastrophe: Myron the stout emerging from the pee place,
uplifting his zipper.

Is there room in Catskill for two golden Aphrodites?
No more than in Khoni for two mammoth Myrons.

I struck his throat with a longing such as Mother
strikes the heart. He staggered back to the beer vendor,
thrusting aside with great fatty arms all in his way.

I approached Stanley short sleeves and Lennie pursed lips. I said, "Let us repair to the device of false thrill and pretend to fill our lives with meaning."

Stanley short sleeved said, "What?"

I found myself sheathed in unaccountable moisture; a stench had supplanted my divine perfume – these horrors had driven from my mind the need to translate my every poetic note into Myron-speak.

I restated: "Let's go ride the Cyclone, you assholes."

Queued for the ride, I slandered my new friends' manliness at a volume all Khoni could hear. I was stylishly repulsive; they loved me; they never doubted my identity.

Bear-lugging Stanley said, "After we close this place we should head over to Sheepshead Bay and go out on one of those night-fishing boats."

Lennie pursed lips said, "Sure. The only thing my wife would like better than me staying out all night would be me coming home with a bucket of smelly fish."

Stanley said, "I'm talking blues. They're worthy foes."

I did not believe my task could be achieved atop Poseidon's mighty tides. How might Myron remain earthbound? I said, "Why don't we just buy them. That would save a lot of time, and would probably be a lot cheaper too."

Stanley short sleeves said, "What's wrong with you? Did Minnie
give you a curfew?"

My godly pride nearly departed my control –
the messenger of love knows no limits save those
of the new chains of Father. And, of course,
every whim of the golden goddess of love.

I had to brake and recall I was mortal for the day. I said, "Who's
carrying the bear of guilt? Not me. In my house, curfew is
when I get home."

My first mortal mistake. Stanley had declared against
returning home. It was imperative that I know why.
Repeatedly disparaging him might only bury his motive.

Punishment was swift: I was taken by a whirl of confusion.
As I baited Stanley short sleeves before the blazing Cyclone,
I concurrently saw myself in a self-propelled vehicle.
A large door rose along the ceiling; I glided forward
into a small, stark room. A dog barked, yet
I did not bludgeon it. A two-wheeled vehicle,
mostly spokes, fell. I cursed: "Michael!"
Who is Michael?

A woman appeared, offered her cheek; I kissed it,
braced for her swoon. Instead she asked about milk,
dry cleaning (pounding clothes on dusty rocks?).
A shiny white bag was handed me; I walked out a door.
Though I did her bidding, I felt no more passion for her
than she for me. What benumbed hell was this?

The snailish queue allowed me time to crack this conundrum:
when I duplicated Myron's flabby form I likewise
duplicated his flabby mind. They would no more readily part
than salt from water.

Eternal vigilance alone would keep the great wooden horse
of his insipid thoughts from wreaking havoc
inside my deathless soul. This was not alarmist –
already I craved the wretched tube food.

Riders of the storm

Stanley short sleeves departed to a telephone;
whom would he contact but Eileen, the intended
of the bear? I could not permit a success; my task
was growing too complex. How might Odysseus' journey
have complicated had he phoned Penelope along the way?

I too exited, to confer with Utilitas, son of Zeus,
and god of thunderbolts through wires. I asked
that he thwart Stanley short sleeves' communications
throughout the evening.

When I made to return, the god of current,
direct and alternating, said, *"Why such haste? You could linger
hours, by our time, without a second passing below;
Lord Helios will delay the chariot a single step,
and all time on earth, and the devices that measure it,
will correct to our leisure."*

I was happy to accede.

He said, *"You are fortunate to be a courier of love.
I change every traffic light on this smog-blanketed world.
Where is fulfillment, save in inconveniencing
the greatest number of vehicles? Mortals do not
suspect my existence; according to their science
my task is impossible."*

I said I smelled a godly prank. He ran proud fingers along
his wire garland. He said, *"Years ago I intimated*
to the learned elite that the speed of light and electricity
is finite. So desperate were they to be relieved of the infinite —
for which their minds are not fashioned — it became their canon.
Now, in educated circles, to demur is to powder yourself
in flour and call yourself a biscuit."

The god of copper and optical fibers turned solemn.
He said, *"Prometheus stole fire from the heavens*
and handed it to mortals. It was sacrilege. With
my misinformation I ensured there will be
no further intrusion into the holiness of light."

I said, *"Surely they will see their error. Technology abounds here."*

Utilitas crepitated with laughter. He said, *"You are new*
on the pay-phone-studded earth. Once mortals establish
a truth, they will defend it as a bear her cubs.
Thousands of years ago, they decided there was but one god.
Shall you and I — verily! that's two gods! — toast to them?"

So we did. I returned to the Cyclone; my absence
had not been noticed.

Lennie pursed lips nudged my ballast with an elbow. He said,
"Check out this chick."

The clothing of Khoni women conceals only the pink parts,
where Aphrodite rules – though nothing could more
offend her sense of beauty. All other skin is left
to Helios's rays, which char it olive-picker brown.
I cannot imagine a man's hand, even fat and sweaty as mine,
reaching in desire to such despoiled flesh.

Greater my horror when I saw the specimen
Lennie pursed lips chose – a beast from beyond
the lip of the world. Still, as Myron,
I had to stand and face it.

Lennie pursed lips said, "Look at those legs. Look at those
shoulders. There goes my ulcer."

Could great sculptor Praxiteles have ever grown
so weak of sight, dry of loins, unsteady of mind
that he sculpted a woman, yet imposed her onto a man
so powerful that mighty Heracles would hesitate
to challenge him? Lennie pursed lips' inamorata
was a woman of such musculature, such definition
of vein and sinew, such breadth of shoulder
and power of back, thigh, and chest, that but for
the teal patches astride her nipples, no one could guess that
here is a woman. For all this, people did not scatter
at her approach; few seemed to notice her.

Stanley short sleeves returned. Lennie pursed lips said, "Look at
that babe in the green bikini."

I said, "Does she transport you to the temple of Aphrodite? – I
mean, does she hoist your bone?"

Said Stanley short sleeves, "I'm not into women who look more like a man than I do."

Lennie pursed lips said, "Let's go talk to her."

Stanley said, "And say what? We're three middle-aged guys who thought we'd come over here and try to say something clever. Even though you could beat the hell out of all of us without breaking a sweat."

Lennie pursed lips said, "Why not? A few years ago we would have gone over there."

Stanley short sleeves said, "Who are you kidding? We've never approached a woman, not since college, not in twenty-five years."

My godly vanity twinged. I said, "I'm not the type to score and tell."

Bear-swinging Stanley put an arm around my sunken shoulders. He said, "Myron, you're a talented guy and a good provider. But score? Come on. Let's all admit it's not on our resumés."

Lennie's lips rolled in opposition. He said, "Don't tell me you wouldn't love to peel a couple of those bikinis."

Stanley short sleeves said, "I like looking as much as the next guy. Well, maybe not if you two were the next guys. But this is just talk. Correct me if I'm wrong."

An important discovery: Stanley, bent on tarrying,
did not harbor, or at least did not betray, ambitions of infidelity.

Then what was keeping him from home? I sensed it was more
than fraternity.

What would Myron respond? I had had but one flash
of his tepid kiss; tepid an adulterer does not make;
though tepid at home does not mean tepid away.

I said, "Why does a choir boy like you come out at all? Aren't
you afraid of temptation?"

He said, "There are other things beside temptation."

Woe that the gate to the Cyclone opened before he expounded;
I might have learned him right then. We were secured
in our cars, bear between.

The car lurched and began the long rise. Now my opportunity
to enter Khoni in true Catskillian fashion. Apollo appears
with a blaze of light no eye can withstand; Poseidon
shakes the earth so mighty peaks quake, great cities tremble,
and stoutest vessels succumb to lashing seas.
I departed for another conference with Utilitas,
then an unnoticed return.

Immediately below us, Myron the stout lumbered once more
from beer stand to bathroom. Certain that he was beside them,
his friends did not recognize him. What worse for mortals
than a dram of knowledge?

The ocean spread before us, Poseidon's fingers
fondling the long beach. A majestic tower stood like
a grateful offering for many safe arrivals. Shores
far across the water flared like burning fields.

At the acme our car bumped to a halt; when Myron's
gravity-absorbent body saw the drop ahead, fear from his mind
jolted through mine. As I arranged, Utilitas extinguished
all electricity in Khoni; the inversion from blazing frenzy
to silent darkness was profound.

Atop the Cyclone, mortals were beyond each other's designs.

Stanley short sleeves said, "What a view! They should turn out
the lights more often."

He did not comprehend. Immense ominous clouds,
illumined by the city behind, formed with unearthly speed;
the wind stiffened. Lennie pursed lips pointed and said, "We
better get going or we're going to get fried up here."

There was no exit; Utilitas held us firm. An offshore gale
caused the Cyclone to groan, like a great beast vexed.
Stanley and Lennie scrutinized the structure for signs of give.
Rain began. Moist-pate Stanley opened his shirt and
draped one wing over the bear.

The power of Catskill now descended. Lightning
like umbrella ribs silenced the mortals;
it was resonant Squall, pealing apprentice
to father Zeus. Another burst, and another,
in furious repetition, each lighting the park brighter
than a bleached noon desert, then plunging it into
ever blacker blackness.

Squall leashed so rapid a sequence that Khoni appeared
under a divine strobe, all movement frozen in frames.
Lennie pursed lips whimpered; Stanley short sleeves

lifted his feet from the car floor, as if that
would stanch a lightning strike from a purposeful god.
He had lost all reason.

The black in the park below was otherworldly;
thousands of mortals in piscine proximity
made no sound. When it was over I said, "That was in-fucking-
credible."

A long moment passed before the others, doubled low
over the restraining bar, hands rigid and white,
could talk. Stanley short sleeves said, "Is everybody all right?"

Lennie pursed lips said, "Do I still exist? Touch me."

I said, "That one's on you."

Bear-bearing Stanley said, "Now I know what it is to feel the
power of god."

I was thunderstruck that he could so quickly
divine my essence through this facing of fat.
I said, as would Myron, "I didn't know you were into god."

He said, "I'm talking about El Niño." I requested dilation. He
said, "Don't you remember those extraordinary storms? 'El
Niño' is the Christ child."

I said, "And this is what you mean by feeling the power of god?

"What did you think I meant?"

It was well I was on a mission of love; else this blasphemy
would demand redress. Squall lacked my forgiveness.
From a cloud dropped a flurry of lightning bolts which
did not vanish, but instead stuck like brachiate fire
in the water's surface. They began to spin, flattening
into a blazing disk with teeth of flame;
after turning on edge, the disk started across the bay.
Water surged as if from the prow of Agamemnon's great ship;
once on land, dunes scattered with similar fury.

Riders trapped atop the Cyclone dispatched hysterical pleas
to god; no talk of El Niño now! Stanley short sleeves
abandoned the bear as he dug for the car floor;
even fealty to his Eileen had limits.
The disk crossed the boardwalk beside the ride,
scorching and splintering planks. I asked
what he thought of divine power now;
I received no answer.

The disk ascended the Cyclone tracks behind us;
I could not suppress the terror pounding through
Myron's overloaded heart. Heat approached; our hair –
what we had of it – tugged from Squall's powerful charge.
We were certain of a swift tryst with Lord Hades.
Mercy that the disk hurdled us and flew back into the sea,
disappearing with the hiss of a hundred serpents.

Utilitas restored power; our car lurched down the drop.
The park below burst back into color and happy tumult;
on the Cyclone there was no bravado. After
the unpleasant centrifugal trial, Stanley short sleeves
and Lennie pursed lips were mute, pale.

The powers I burned to unleash, the proofs of divine dint
I ached to demonstrate upon their temporal bodies!
But I reined myself, lest I compromise my mission —
whose nature, I realized, I still knew little of. I said, "Onward,
fearless riders. We have so many rides and so little vomit."

Twitching Lennie leaned on his ulcer. Stanley short sleeves
searched for an excuse, knowing I would ridicule it.
His sweaty forehead reflected kinetic colors. He said, "What are
you looking at? If I don't want to go on another ride I don't
have to. And that doesn't mean I have to go home yet either. I
don't owe you an explanation."

The Funky-Town sirens

Stanley short sleeves and Lennie pursed lips chaperoned me
onto the sparse boardwalk at park's edge, away
from the parlous rides. Squall had wiped clean the sky;
Selene, goddess of the moon, had begun her rise
from the horizon. It was almost Catskill on earth.

All that lacked was music of the immortal mount.
I summoned Riff, daughter of Terpsichore, muse of sweet sound.
Each boardwalk plank she fixed with a tone dulcet
as a pipe of Pan – passing pedestrians' feet played
the vast marimba. I said to Riff, *"These sounds are euphonious,*
yet desultory. Where is order in your art?"

Fleet-fingered Riff said, *"Did you not desire an earthly sound?*
Many a mortal considers randomness the highest art –
they worship paintings like bird spatters; their finest brush
is a spray can; their public icons are not heroes fallen in war,
but bereted victims of drive-by shootings."

I asked, *"Why do you not chasten mortals for their affront*
to beauty?"

She said, *"Passing one's brief stay on this ugly earth*
never knowing the sublime is the sternest punishment."

I asked that the resumption of punishment be delayed
until my departure. To Riff's direction I spaced
oncoming pedestrians like roller teeth in a music box –

when their feet struck the boardwalk, it played a pastorale.
I thought of Catskill leas and fought back godly tears.

Lennie pursed lips said, "What the hell is that noise?"

Stanley short sleeves jerked his head side to side,
like a rodent. He put an ear to the boardwalk. He said, "It's the
wood. It must be decomposing from the inside."

I said, "But it's pressure-treated against decay."

Rational Stanley said, "The chlorine in the air probably breaks
those compounds down. It's very corrosive. You can hear it for
yourself. What else could it be?"

With a chord of godly dissonance, Riff flew off.
I yearned to go with her.

I took the bear's paw so I could stand before Stanley
and plumb his mind. It was at work – so much I could tell.
Yet I could find no cables from need to redress, from
passion to action, from beauty to suffering. Immortals
read some men so easily: soldiers are obsessed,
simplified by war; why are not lovers equally possessed?
Should they not be?

The heartrace of Squall's spectacle ebbed
in Zephyrus' gentle offshore caress. We reentered
the crowd. Two boys staggered forward, pants suspended
from their pubescent penetralia. Behind them surged forth
Myron, beer radiating from his sallowed skin. Though asphalt
had laid bare his knees, he was determined to rejoin
his friends. I interceded my bulk. He stopped

and blinked at me. He said, "You're the best-looking fucking guy I've seen all day."

This mortal had consumed sufficient alcohol to drop immortal-livered Dionysus; what would it take to halt him? I struck him with the thirst of a salt miner. Squeals of disgust rose from the crowd as he reversed course.

Stanley short sleeves said, "That guy looks just like you. Even the clothes."

I said, "If I knew you were going to check me out I would have worn something more revealing."

Lennie pursed lips said, "You reveal plenty with your clothes on."

Stanley short sleeves said, "And that guy was revealing exactly the same."

Thus Squall's fulgurations, the most spectacular of the millennium, are attributed to a christened stretch of water; Riff's timeless beauty is a matter of wood rot; and two fat men in identically distended clothing are cause for wonder. Here is mortal awe.

An image propelled the thought of Mother upon me; two young women beside us were clad in short dresses so tight that a Greek maiden in a chiton in a gale would look modest beside. The inspiration was not the women themselves; rather their thrusting nipples, obvious in detail, each a circle of deferential forms about a jutting monument of majesty. Just as an aureole –

a breast – a woman – is naught without a nipple,
so is this world pointless without love and its goddess.

The two women were equine, wide of mouth and
robust of tooth. Yet they presented with an enticing blend
of shyness and forthrightness: Had we been on the rides?
Were they fun? Where did we get the bear? Far out!

Had I myself chosen adulterous partners for mortals
unsavory as we, I could not have surpassed them:
more attractive than we but not intimidatingly so,
and unaccountably enthusiastic. Stanley evinced
no interest; I felt only vague discomfort. Lennie
had spoken like a roué; Stanley and I concurred –
we would let him seduce.

Instead, while changing neither form nor position,
Lennie shriveled and fled – I never conceived cowardice
so profound. Merciful Stanley short sleeves stepped forward
and described our ride on the Cyclone.

Sheila pressed palms to cheeks and said, "You're kidding!"
Connie grabbed my thick arm and shrieked, "Get outta here!"

Her touch unnerved me; at once I was red, uncertain,
sweatier still – with a Demosthenes mouthful of marbles.
The conversation fell to Stanley short sleeves, who reveled
in our discomfort. The women glowed at him.

A generation of annual reunions – so Stanley said –
had been free of contact with unknown women;
yet he was so masterful a seduction was his for the asking.

What explained his skill? This: he was indifferent
to the outcome. While Lennie of the quavering lips
and I, his grand companion, were prisoners of fantasies
of young women, stolid Stanley, for reasons
still beyond my divine comprehension, was not.

In Catskill I bedded innumerable immortals; here,
immobilized by my inner Myron, I stared dumbly
at my unfurled feet.

Stanley said, "Ladies, I'd like you to meet quiet Lennie."

Lennie smiled witlessly, hand on his side, ulcer
now a javelin bore. Chariots could have driven through
the breach in conversation. I insisted he speak; at length
he said, "So, you girls live around here?"

Oh, a fiery pit for him! No, for me, if this be the poetry
I inspire! But his response proved more favorable than I knew.
The women live on the Island, as does he: not Melos nor Crete,
but Long Island. They spoke not of oracles nor temples,
but rather, in shared code, of secrets known as LIE and LIRR;
what matter the fodder of love if all share the taste for it?

Now bloomed the desire: Sheila, looking up through
lacquered lashes, laughed when Lennie's grimace
suggested humor; Connie's nails, gleaming like standards
in battlefield sun, touched his arm. He jumped at contact.

I peered, with limited success, into his swirling mind:
the wellheads of his desires were like hot springs scabbed
by their own deposits – still under some middle-aged pressure,
but choked.

If he would depart, I might better learn Stanley.
Then providence appeared: Connie announced a craving
for rum and Coke. I spoke at once: "We'll escort you."

Every ride was in motion. People clutched vats of food
as would bears sniffing first snow. Save for a few puddles,
Squall's awesome display just an hour before
might not have happened; he is accustomed to
rapid disappearance of his work. Mother rarely operates
in ephemeral fashion — what chaos would take
this inconstant earth if she did!

Connie and Sheila asked us into the Beachcomber Bar.
Stanley short sleeves proclaimed uxoriousness,
the incontrovertible excuse. I claimed the same;
he called me hypocrite — did I not deny my curfew?
Strange, since it was he who continued to delay
our departure. Still, I accepted his abuse;
I enjoyed it; I felt more of him with each slap.

Lennie too made apologies. But a moment hence
his mind reversed; he allowed Sheila his arm.
Before the three passed the doors Connie turned back
to Stanley and pressed herself against him. She said,
"What about you?"

Stanley laughed and retreated. He said, "I have to save my
energy. I have a big date tonight."

She said, "You do? Then what are you doing here?"

He said, "I've been through a lot with these guys. Once a year
we get together and try to remember what it was."

I said, "And decide if it wasn't a long mistake."

She said, "If it's a really big date, you should be going."

He said, "Don't worry. I won't miss it."

What could this mean? I derided him, hoping to rise
a legible image in his mind. He laughed at me;
still, I could not read him.

Through the swinging bar door flew flights of
incomprehensible music. I thought of the Sirens,
whose song no man can withstand. If exposed
to what mighty Odysseus could not resist but for ropes
round his chest, I wondered if it would take even thread
to bind the man with the short sleeves.

Connie's parting kiss sent circles of sensation
up my neck. The humiliation! Stanley short sleeves
offered her instead his hand; he was insulated.
He and I turned away.

Lennie pursed lips cried out: " 'Funky Town!' "

Stanley short sleeves and I continued; Lennie pursued us.
He said, "Don't you remember what we used to do to 'Funky
Town'? It's on the juke box in there. Come on."

He began a contortion that I could not help but associate
with battle goring and incipient death. We kept on.
Lennie cursed our old age and disappeared into the bar,
still in demented step.

Stanley and I crossed the boulevard and approached the subway. I said, "So you're ready to head home now?"

He said, "No. But damn if I was going to spend my night listening to 'Funky Town.' "

Into Persephone's maw

It soothed that my task continued among evidence
of immortal forces: the concrete walk, thought eternal as gold
when laid, was moldered by the parade of Seasons.
Persephone, queen of the underworld, had laid vents
over the subway tracks so pedestrians would look down
and think of her – and fear her – and thus honor her.

I was confident the gratings, which resembled the baleen
of a great aquatic beast, would hold even
my mortal weight – to what use would she put
mangled fat? Stanley of the white shirt preferred to tread
the uncertain sidewalk. It was not the goddess
of the everafter he feared; it was city workers
who maintain the metal.

Long yellow ribbons soon funneled us all over the vents.
Just ahead a woman shrieked, grabbed her leg, and fell.
I thought jealous Persephone had seized a toe, intending
to extrude her gorily through the ferocious metal fabric. No,
the woman's high-heel had caught; a shocked foot, bare
but for nylon, had stepped onto cold square steel.
Stanley short sleeves offered a gallant, uninvolved
shoulder as she reshod.

Her heels, frail as hummingbirds' beaks, raised tide
in my heart. Sandaled Mother vested power in such shoes;
women wearing them are more assured, and thus
more alluring.

There is more: high-heels steer women away from
subway grates, shielding them from Persephone's realm;
men, who tread the grates, are naked
to disquieting premonitions of the below.
Such thoughts kill them years sooner than women,
yielding them earlier into the dark goddess' grasp.

Beared Stanley and I descended to the subway trench.
Rows of steel trees supported a rippled convex ceiling;
polished parallel tracks disappeared into infinity.
This masterwork looked to have been scooped by divine dint.

I had planned to press Stanley for his next destination;
instead I said this: "When we were up on the Cyclone I asked
if you were into god. What would it take for you to see the
hand of a god on earth?"

Stanley said, "Did you say: the hand of god? Or the hand of *a*
god? Just how bizarre are you going to get with this?"

As Utilitas averred: They will cling to the certainty
of one god, though a moment of thought reveals this planet
far too large and untidy a job. I said, "A god, any god, whatever."

He said, "Do you realize that in all the years I've known you
this is the first time I've heard you use the word 'god' without
'damn' right after it?"

I repeated. He said, "You're serious? All right. If I won the New
York lottery, the New Jersey lottery, and the Connecticut lottery
on the same day. Maybe."

I said, "So it's a matter of long odds." He shook his head. I said,
"What if I predict the time the next train comes."

He said, "Fine. Make it soon."

I made an undetectable exit to confer with Transitas
(first cousin to Utilitas), god of subways: IRT, BMT, IND,
and, erratically, PATH. Upon my return
I showed Stanley short sleeves my watch; at the second
of my forecast, the D train rolled in.

Stanley said, "Why don't you always do this? I've wasted half
my life down here."

He made for the car door, but I held him back. I said, "The next
one will be here soon. It will have only women on it."

He said, "Great. It won't smell of urine."

A train rolled slowly through the station. Women sat,
women stood by the poles, women leaned against the doors,
women of all ages, races, and dress – and not one man.
Stanley short sleeves trotted beside the train and
studied every car.

He said, "How the hell did you know that was going to happen?
What was it, a convention?"

Within a minute came another – my first earthly inspiration.
All ten cars were filled with water clear as the Aegean;
in them swam clouds of fish: lapidary reef dwellers
in small schools peering myopically out the windows;
satanic rays baring jagged mouths ripped from their bellies;

sharks with teeth fearsome as Father's, indolent and content
among their upcoming meals; ethereal jellyfish, identical
with their own shades.

Stanley cried, "The doors! The doors — we'll drown!"

He made to flee, but I held him; he was too terrified to realize
my immortal strength.

Unseen by disabled Stanley, Transitas rode the back
of the departing train. I applauded his feat; he said
it was the work of Aquarius — also son of Poseidon —
god of fountains, aquariums, and terrariums.
I protested terrariums are not all watery. Transitas said,
"Nothing exalts him as does the orange newt."

It took no godly sensitivity to hear Stanley's pounding heart.
His pupils were Kalamata olives, his complexion
Catskill run-off. With delight I awaited his
mortal rationalization of my immortal deed.

At length he said, "The train had to be on the way to the
Aquarium. It's the next stop on this line. Had to be."

He looked at me piteously; I vouchsafed mercy
and held my words.

We boarded the next train. I hoped doubt and unease
would ferment the dense vat of his mind, sending
his true ambitions, like grape skins, to the surface,
where I might skim them. He stared at the window
across the car; beside his reflection sat a man in a suit of fat,
which never failed to horrify me.

The wheels rumbled against the rails, jostling my dank body.
I experienced a new feeling: not fury, which insists
on instantaneous redress; this was more constant, less vital.
It was earthly. It was irritation.

I said, "What do you want to do now?" He declared no
ambition. I said, "What's going on? Trouble at home?"

Another impatient error: I snatched for the pearl,
and felt his valves close on me.

He said, "I'll tell you what. We didn't go fishing, so let's get off
the train a few stops early, in midtown. What if we get home a
couple of hours late? We go straight home every damn day of
our lives."

What had I wrought?

Dance of the pudding

The subway is magnificent as any temple. Mortals of Greece
carved exquisite edifices, but of modest scale, for the select;
mortals of this teeming city bored through rock as hard,
for hundreds of miles, for the daily millions!

Transitas tells its tale:
Step Lively, son of Poseidon, fought to extend family dominion
to earth's rocky surface; he was defeated. He dared not return
without a pelt for his father's cruel eyes; thus
he annexed this thin layer between world and underworld.
Savage Poseidon sends ships to the bottom for the pleasure
of watching mortals die; Step Lively plotted similar evil:
he fitted subway turnstiles with scything blades so mortals
would pay their toll in flesh. Lightning-wielding Zeus
vaporized the cruel devices; Transitas, his son, assumed control
of the underground passages.

Step Lively waited two generations in the Times Square station,
in full view, in full Olympian regalia – no mortal thought
that sight unusual – until trains required replacement
and stations refurbishment. He infiltrated their design:
turnstiles have no blades, but are narrower than the old;
obese mortals must squeeze through in humbling fashion.

Inside the new trains lies Step Lively's masterstroke:
seats are sculpted to cup the nates, but differ in measure.
The ridge ostensibly separating seats instead lodges
in the full flesh of unsuspecting hams, often thrusting a rider

lapward of the rider beside, or embeds in the cleft
between the cheeks – as immobilizing as a Spartan blade
across the sinew named for fearless Achilles.

Where is the outrage? Cunning Step Lively learned
that pride among mortals is vast but fragile. To decry
this torment would be to demand: Fit my great hams!

Step Lively dreamed of seats as Procrustean guides –
a million nates would feel his rising scythe;
all overflowing flesh, train loads of it, would be offered
for sacrifice at Catskill.

Said Father Zeus: *"When immortals feel honored
by incineration of fat fannies, immortality itself will end."*

Thus his judgement: Poseidon's base son left the subway forever;
but conductors will forever call his name – Step Lively –
as train doors close.

Appetite intruded upon my bloody thoughts; again
I craved tube food. No words bespeak the revulsion.

Into the swaying car appeared Beggasus, god
of the magical cup, which refills each day without effort,
like an oasis spring.

Then entered a well-dressed man. He called, "*Street News*!
Latest issue. Stories about the homeless, by the homeless, for
the homeless. Poetry by men of the streets, and by Norman
Mailer. One dollar. We ain't criminals. Help us help ourselves.
Just one dollar."

Stanley purchased a copy. I said, "Do you really want to know
about the life of the homeless?"

He said he could not be indifferent to their awful plight.
I asked was it not more compassionate to elevate the spirit
of their stratum than degrade all others to meet it. I said, "You
could give him a copy of *The Odyssey* instead of a dollar. It
might change his life forever."

He said, "A dollar buys more comfort. Be realistic."

I said, "What if he was selling Homer? Would you buy one of
his works?"

He said, "I read Homer in college. Wonderful stuff, as I recall.
But why would I need two copies?"

How did I fortify myself to go on?

Among forty mortals in our car sat six colossal women.
One was encased in that same Protean fabric as the woman
who earlier eclipsed Helios. I directed my divine nose
toward her; I detected nothing. A woman without scent
is not possible. The high-hemmed fashions of
Connie and Sheila ventilated as a dog sprays an oak,
but this woman chose to shield her bouquet.

With gargantuan displacement and absent scent,
she was destined for solitude; what man would desire her?
Like the others, she rode with eyes down, as though
they would as soon combust as meet another's.

Alas, I had misread another mortal. Suddenly she looked
toward us; she had seen through my adipose disguise
and was beholding my majesty. No! She fixed instead
on Stanley short sleeves. She stared unrelentingly,
unashamedly. When the sun daily rises no one takes notice;
but a comet, a far dimmer but rarer light, causes sensation:
so, to me, was this unadulterated love-look
in the grimy subterranean box.

Tess with the arms like loofahs smiled at Stanley short sleeves
and pointed to the seat beside him. He lifted the stuffed bear.
When she sat, the seat divider could no more contain
her thighs than the leaves of the quaking aspen hold back
the north wind. Stanley did not look at her;
in the realm of Transitas, mortals do not acknowledge
those unknown.

Tess loofah arms transgressed at once. She said, "My, that's a
beautiful animal. Where did you find it?"

Startled Stanley said Khoni. She wondered if he had rung
the bell atop the tall pole with the sledge. His eyes
searched for a safe direction. He said it was nothing,
just dropping a few bottles.

I said, "Twice! He did it twice! No one else could do it once."

She felt his bicep and nodded. She said, "The bottles had no
chance."

An aspect of alarm appeared.

Tess loofah arms said, "I had a lover who was too shy to tell me how he felt about me – you wouldn't believe how intimidated men are of large sensual women. So he wrote notes and pinned them to the paws of teddy bears, and then he sent me the teddy bears. Is that what you are going to do?"

Stanley short sleeves said, "Yes, that's right. This one is for my wife."

Tess loofah arms sighed; she leaned more weight against him. She said, "I love men who admit that they adore their wives. That is so romantic. Are you going to make love when you get home?"

I thought of Myron the Stout, overrunning a Khoni urinal, and how he would have savored the distress.

Damp Stanley said, "That's quite a personal question."

Tess loofah arms said, "I'm sorry. I forget that some people are very embarrassed about their love life."

Embarrassed Stanley said, "I'm not embarrassed. Yes, that's exactly what I plan to do when I get home."

Tess loofah arms said, "If I were going to lie down with you — well! — I certainly wouldn't be embarrassed. I'd tell everyone. But I'm afraid you would be ashamed to admit that. I mean with me."

Stanley insisted she had said this hypothetically. She replied, "What is the hypothetical? Just the real asking for a chance to happen."

She let him steep in the brilliance of her remark;
Mother could not have done better. At length Tess said,
"Is your wife slender?"

Stanley said, "Yes, I would say so."

She said, "How about her hips. Same?"

He nodded with foreboding. She said, "So you fit comfortably
in her cradle."

He was stunned into silence. Why was he submitting
to her questions?

Tess loofah arms said, "I've always thought that the way a man's
hips fit into your cradle is what matters most in love. If there
isn't a good fit, well, there's not a lot you can do. I am large, but
I have been complimented on my structure, the way that men
fit with me."

At last I felt the twinge of escape reflex in his legs.

She said, "Have you ever betrayed your wife?"

He said, "It never even occurred to me."

She said, "Women must flirt with you. You're very attractive.
I'm sure you've heard that many times."

She slung a monumental thigh over his; her loofah-arm,
thrust behind his neck, buried his nose in the bear's pate.
Sister Phobos, goddess of dread, streaked through the car.

Tess said, "Let me show you my love, just once. I will have you
back to your wife on time. And I swear you will never forget
me."

Her passion thrilled me. Stanley neared a swoon; but
he had not seen the end: a woman approached,
mighty as Tess, with skin the color of a great pyre
the day after. Unlike Tess, rounded like a sitting hen,
Shameeka queen of thrust cantilevered in bust and butt;
yet she was perfectly balanced, and walked the shimmying car
without support. I gave her my seat; Stanley
was secured between them.

Thrusting Shameeka said to pale Stanley, "What you got under
the bear? Looks like you're hiding something good."

He clutched the bear tightly to his lap. He said, "What do you
mean? There's nothing under it."

Shameeka queen of thrust spoke to Tess loofah arms
behind his head.

She said, "I like them modest, girlfriend. Turns me on."

She held up her hand, which Tess slapped. Their upper arms
did the dance of the pudding. Shameeka said to Stanley, "I
know you like a big woman, 'cause I hear you talking with my
sister here. Let me tell you something, sweet vanilla — a black
woman got everything a white woman does. Some say we got
more."

Tess loofah arms said, "What might that be?"

Royal Shameeka smiled and said, "I'd be happy to demonstrate.
Then we'll let the man choose the fairest."

Tess said, "I think it would be barbaric to make this beauty
choose between goddesses like us. Why don't we share?"

Just then the train stopped at the Atlantic Avenue station.
Stanley short sleeves oozed free of his wards like
the innards of a blown egg. He pushed out the door;
the bear bounced against his hamstrings as he vanished
down the platform.

★

Millennia ago, when Greeks set proud Troy to the torch,
Pallas Athena might have whisked wily Odysseus
straight home to Penelope and Ithaca. I could so take
Stanley short sleeves; it would require little
to figure his abode and transport him. Yet wise Athena allowed
full twenty years before Odysseus climbed exhausted
from gray water onto his native dirt. I had thought
Athena arrogant to arrogate these decades, a quarter
of the warrior's span on the planet, against his will.

Now I reconsidered.

Had wise Athena given much-enduring Odysseus a choice —
lie with perfect Calypso, Circe, and the rest, and then
return to constant Penelope, or go instead straight to her —
would he not have chosen just as the gods did for him?

What mortal would cede those years of passion —
suspecting that when he did return, his wife would again
be his?

As Stanley short sleeves bolted into the Brooklyn night
his gait suggested more than fear of six hundred pounds
of predatory women. If his draw home was potent
he would have remained on the subway, stalwart.
There was more afoot in his soft soul. I was sure of it.

I believe in the divine law of poetry: Had Zeus-born Athena
wanted a world without verse she would have
dispatched Odysseus home; without his trials
there would have been no mortal impulse to lyricism:
this boot-trodden earth would have remained prosaic
for all time. Yet there is poetry — albeit mostly bad —
everywhere about. However obscure Mother has been
about my challenge here, through Stanley short sleeves
I was destined to contribute my lines.

First blood

I climbed from Transitas' fluorescent realm
into the domain of quick-zipping Urinus; he appears
in all lands — against trees, walls, and corners,
in snow banks and on outgoing fires. By outraging
the most stoic of noses, he speeds lagging laborers home.

The sky was gray. Helios and his pastel minions were gone,
but Night had not taken possession with her full huelessness.
The unbounded stars did not transmit; the sky
sagged with soot to the building crests. It would take
sky-ruling Zeus a flick to clear the ether so
the city could absorb the Olympian wisdom inscribed above.
Was this permanent punishment, or timed for my sojourn?

A buzz, a burst of light: a modern constellation.
Such was Father Zeus' answer: wanting
the sky's diamond vertices, mortals of the city
draw their own images in neon —
in the place of Leo the Lion sat Red Dog the Beer.

One block away Stanley short sleeves stood
beneath a street light, heaving, absently grooming the bear.
I asked after his cowardly flight; did he not
have a big date later tonight? He replied that
his arrival would be of little use if in inanimate condition.

He said, "You know, if I died on that train, Eileen would have been left destitute. I'm sure my insurance policy wouldn't cover being crushed to death that way."

I said it was too bad she wasn't here. He said, "Think so?"

He smiled; she was at play in his mind. I pursued her. I said, "What do you think she would have done when she saw you disappear under that thigh?"

He said, "I'm not sure she would have done anything." I said I did not believe it. He said, "What could she do? She would have been giving away a good quarter-ton. Anyway, I think she would say that if I wanted to get to her badly enough, I would find a way."

I said, "And don't you?"

He did not respond; I feared she would depart. I said, "How long is it you're married?"

He said, "A strange question from my best man."

I said, "I don't remember when I was best man."

He said, "Eight years last month."

I said, "Eight years? Is that all? You shouldn't be avoiding your wife until well into your second decade."

He said there had never been a day he had not anticipated his return home. What was I talking about?

I said then this was the first day. He pitied my confusion:
perhaps I was the one with reason to avoid home?

His remark set Myron's rabid recall on me:
it was the plump, pleasant-looking woman with thin lips
and blonde curly hair who had greeted me earlier. Minnie.
I stood beside her, in even more portly form than
I knew myself to be. Why see myself this way?
My image was refracted through the lens
of slender Stanley.

I rotated Minnie. She was round and full, pleasing;
but aged and content. She was indifferent to passion;
we had not shared it in many cycles.

It was the passion of Stanley and Eileen I needed to learn.
I said, "Why did you tell that monstress you were going home
to make love with your wife? As if Eileen will be waiting up for
you."

He said, "Why are you so interested in my sex life? Could it be
because you don't have one any more?"

A dagger to my head! Could the mortal read me, even
as he rendered me illiterate? Myron's irrepressible thoughts
had Minnie and me in bed; I seized her compressible
upper arms, pulled her to me, kissed her roughly.
Our round bodies melded, as two butting soap bubbles
pop and become one larger one. Yet it was an ancient image,
a palimpsest beneath my impassive life.

Compounding my wretchedness was another scene:
Minnie and I, a younger Stanley, and a woman –
small, dark, pretty, laughing – walking
the litter-strewn sand below the wooden walk of Khoni.
Young beauties of all dimension, browned and
in near total exposure, paraded. My eyes could not help
but follow their paths; my heart was desolate;
my hand went slack to free it of Minnie's.

Stanley embraced his wife, was content. All these years later
I still felt contempt for him, that he was so simple, that
the same woman commanded every recess of his heart.

Yet I envied him. What exactly did I envy? I hoped
it was only that red blood continued to course
through his union.

Again apprehension echoed through Myron's great volume –
it might be her I wanted: this dark and pretty woman,
this Eileen, who laughed and watched. If it were so,
how would his appetites threaten my godly mission
when she stood before me, which she was certain to do
before the next touch of Aurora's pink pointer?

The Nubian

Street lights dully overlooked the sooty evening. Utilitas'
reciprocating signal commanded all. The driver of a van
emblazoned with a white lily – Mother's favorite bloom –
slowed so the red would bring him to a halt. Unaccountable,
in this speedy city, until I saw a female passenger accost
his neck with ready lips. His chin freely lifted –
a rare scene of sensual mortal happiness.

Alas, he held a cup of steaming drink, forgotten –
until it emptied onto his thigh. He screamed;
the tires screamed; the truck hurtled ahead.

A car, beckoned by Utilitas' green, approached
from the perpendicular, collision imminent. The van driver
tore two-handed at his wheel, cursing with heroic rage.
The van navigated a long skid that narrowly spared the auto,
then departed his control, spinning across the pebbled asphalt,
to shrieks from deepest hell. After metal-bending concussion
with the railing at the subway entrance, the van door
flew open; flowers cascaded into the domain of
many-tokened Transitas. I had not seen as wondrous
a display since the wedding of Tremblas and Adamantine.

A leak ignited, sealing the stairs with a fence of flame.
The lovers debarked hurriedly. The driver's lip sprayed blood
as he screamed that she had cost his job. In terms
melding boudoir and gutter, she replied he could not
withstand her erotic power.

What did Stanley make of such feminine initiative?
I began to ask. Instead my mouth said this: "What a bonanza!
The MTA has a huge action against the florist for destruction
of property and interruption of service. And the driver has an
action against the woman."

My suspicions were now confirmed – through Myron's
plaque-choked heart ran the ichor of Litigius,
bastard son of Ares and Pansy. Litigius loves conflict, but
unlike his father has no stomach for blood. Riding
a Mercedes chariot, armed with briefcase rather than sword,
he faces adversaries not in person but by interrogatory,
aiming not for their lives but their possessions, to leave them
in penury instead of rout, himself with body unscathed,
conscience clear, and wallet full. Myron's life's aim is
to get the pelt – not in battle, but by judgement.

What more formidable foe could beard the son
of the goddess of passion? Yet Janus-like, we shared
a body. For the briefest moment I was grateful for its
vast volume.

Stanley short sleeves said, "How are we going to get out of
here? There are no cabs in this part of Brooklyn."

I said nothing, lest Myron unduly influence him;
a compass will not find true north if repeatedly jostled.

At length he said, "Subways usually run along the avenues. Let's
follow this one until the next stop. How far can it be?"

We began up the broken-metered street;
diminishing tremblings detected by my overlarge feet

told me he was wrong, that we were heading away
from the neighboring station; we and the iron track
quickly parted. He did not face the crisis like
mortal heroes of whom I had heard, who accept
absurd odds and reject all aid. Stanley attempted
to intercept passersby on the plunder-busy street with an
"Excuse me." He was too tentative, his rhythm too slow.

At the next corner our journey was transformed: we faced
an extraordinary mortal, as surely the watchman of the ghetto
as Cerberus guards the underworld. Beer in hand, he lazed
on a full-length chaise set on the concrete walk. A music box
at his side issued repulsive rhythmic rodomontade
on submission and emission.

He had a slave's physique, powerful and venous, graceful
even in repose. Obsidian spectacles occulted his eyes;
only the reflection of lamplight above provided focus. Others
on the street showed tattoos of barbed wire on their biceps;
he wore gold bands around neck and wrists, heavy and rough –
slave chains, now displayed in derision. Why? does the impala
flaunt stripes of a lion's swipe? Or had his beauty,
like mine, incited a jealous father? Though he was
to Stanley short sleeves and Myron as the towering seaside pine
is to tangled scrub, he had wrapped his mighty-boned head
with a bandanna in the manner of a menial.
This was the curse of Nubus.

The Nubian watched us as a cheetah considers chipmunks.
Stanley short sleeves offered a greeting; the Nubian
held an indifferent hand to his ear; it was to us to approach.
Such was the tenor of the scene that he, and we too,
might have expected us to do so on our knees, if not
for the broken glass and inseminated rubber on the ground.

He greeted us: "Gentlemen. Bear."

Stanley said, "Can you tell us where the next station is on the
D line?"

The Nubian said, "The D line? No wheels?"

Stanley short sleeves said, "We came down on the subway. We
thought it would be quicker."

The Nubian held out his hands, as if to say: But here you are.
Stanley said, "Next time we'll know better. But now we need
the subway."

The Nubian said, "I don't like to be going down there. Low
class of people."

I could not control the roiling of my soul; Myron
was besting me over and again. I said, "Who are you? What are
you doing out here on the street?"

The Nubian looked at me over his glasses; he was,
he said, Boss of Bed-Stuy.

Stanley tugged on the rear of my garment. Too late —
a waft drew my godly nose toward the modest bag

beside the Nubian. Eureka! Bouquet of alkaloid and solvent
leaked from many tiny containments. Long
have I known that gay Bacchus, bored with his vintage,
begot Crackus, who surpassed his father's
slumberous narcotic with these: cocaine and ether –
stimulant surpassing and anaesthetic nonpareil.

I announced my intent to do business. The Nubian
directed me to Atlantic Avenue, or Flatbush. I insisted
I buy from him; he asked whether he seemed a store.
I said I smelled product, and I had cash. Stanley's eyes widened;
but he would not now physically remove me, so alien
had I instantly become.

I said, "What don't you like, my color or the color of my
money?"

The Nubian said, "I ain't selling nothing. But say I was. This
shit ain't no pinch between your cheek and gum. You be ending
up in the morgue and I got the man up my ass."

Stanley short sleeves overcame his revulsion
and yanked me away. He said, "Am I getting this right? You
think this man is a crack dealer, and not only are we still
standing here, but you're trying to make a purchase? Do I have
that right?"

His inadvertent grip was doing injury to the innocent bear. I
said, "Have you ever tried crack?"

He said, "Have I ever tried it? No, I haven't tried it. I haven't
tried plunging red-hot pokers into my eyes either. Why are we
discussing this?"

I said, "You're the one who said it. Look at our lives: we go to work, we come home, we watch the tube. The god looking over us is named Tedious. Crack might lift us out of it. Why not?"

He said, "Are you in some psychotic episode? You used to be the most boring man I know. I didn't realize how much I would miss that."

I said, "We might love it; we might not. That's freedom. What else do we have?"

He said, "I have no illusion of being free. And if I did, going home in some brain-fried stupor would not be my exercise of choice."

I thought of Catskill. I said, "For a few minutes you might know how it feels to be on top of the world looking down. A whole new angle on your life. Think how great that would be."

He said, "Looking down on the whole world for you used to mean sitting on top of the Cyclone with two hot dogs in your nose. Now, are you coming, or am I leaving you here?"

I said the drugs didn't seem to be affecting the Nubian any. Stanley with the whitening face said that snakes inject poison into their prey and then eat it; it doesn't bother them either.

I savored that image. In the mind of the Nubian was another, which I readily read: a yellow cab was driving down a wide avenue. Atop its roof stood Stanley and I, each with a grasp of the other's tie, which tightened

as we struggled for balance. Who let go first did not matter;
we would both hurtle into traffic.

I approached the Nubian and said, "You are a noble specimen,
and worthy of an explanation of your condition. Had birth
favored you with skin like mine you would live
in a beautiful home; your work would be far more lucrative,
less strenuous, and legal. Yet this will never be."

The Nubian spat a dart of beer on the ground; dust
sprayed my shoe.

I said, "Once lived a god named Nubus, who ruled all Africa
but lusted for more. Father Zeus parried his relentless challenges
because he loved him. One day, before the ranks of gods,
Nubus proclaimed he would create the mightiest of all waters:
his great body straddled his continent and he peed the river Nile.
Zeus then whisked the immortals to Gibraltar and
from there peed west, his torrent becoming the Atlantic Ocean –
engulfing even his own continent, Atlantis. Every god –
save for Nubus – was properly warned by
the ferocity of his sacrifice.

"Nubus conquered Zeus' lovers and flaunted them – to no effect;
for the lightning god, amours attained are amours forgotten.
At the Olympian council Nubus called Zeus unworthy:
he had abandoned females, gods and mortals alike, unsatisfied,
undone. Had not Nubus proven himself suited to
the thunder-hurler's seat by completing those essential tasks?
He drew out his ebony anatomy and laid it on the council table;
would the father of gods dare do the same?

"Headstrong Nubus had blundered for all eternity; immortal Zeus
rules male genitals as surely as Aphrodite commands mounds.
His own can transfigure easily as his great body does,
easily as water takes the form of a vessel – and can fill
a large vessel indeed. While Nubus admired himself,
Zeus had Hephaestus secure him in chains
which cannot be broken.

"Zeus said, 'Nubus, great among Olympians, you have succumbed
to ambition, many times though I warned you against it.
What had you to gain, save more turd-rotting turf on
this tragic earth? Your supreme insult to me, to Olympus,
will never be reprised. Thus I condemn your progeny
to be at war forever. Some will be torn from their beds
by their own brothers and sold into slavery. When
they are liberated, their burdens will grow worse still:
families will splinter, addictive substances will blight
mere children, and they will wreak terrible crime,
most hideously on one another. When you send prophets
to raise your people from hopelessness and superstitions,
they will be ignored or murdered; some external agent
will always bear the blame for your evil. You, Nubus,
will spend time eternal spading graves for your own victims.' "

Stanley short sleeves said to the Nubian, "Pardon us. My friend
has been under a lot of stress. I'll be taking him to an institution
now."

The Nubian stood, sounding of that same muted clang of gold
which now fills my ears with every stir. He said, "OK, I hear
your rap, now I got a rap for you. Two honkies show up on my
corner with no appointment and be dogging my business. This
corner, this be my office. Everybody know that. You come

through my reception area when you turn off the avenue. That
ain't no pay phone, it be my switchboard. You be acting like
I'm ignorant. You don't show me no respect. Where you get off,
telling me how to be?"

Stanley short sleeves said, "We'll pay for the business we drove
away. How much?"

The Nubian said, "I could take it all. Easy."

I said, "And you deny the curse of Nubus?"

Sister Phobos flashed through the night; it was not
the Nubian I feared. It was Myron, whose influence on me
I could not suppress. How could I learn Stanley short sleeves
when I could not contain my own provocations?

Stanley stared at me with wonder as the Nubian grabbed my
arm. I said, "What's this? Crime? Millions for defense, but not
one cent for tribute!"

Stanley short sleeves cried, "Shut up!"

The Nubian tossed me against a parked car. I stung him
as a spider would; though he looked to be assaulting me
he was paralyzed and toppling. Stanley ran into the street.
There were people in hailing distance, but
he did not hail them. Who would side with us
against the Boss of Bed-Stuy?

He ran back and yelled at the Nubian: "I'll give you my wallet
and my watch. Anything. Don't hurt him."

In his numbed condition the Nubian could not accept;
chalky-lipped Stanley had no way of knowing. With
loosening bowels, he pulled back the Nubian's shoulder
and swung. It was good fortune for Stanley that he forgot
he held the bear; the stuffed animal, not a fist,
bounced against the Nubian's powerful face.

Enough! I cast a mist over the scene; Stanley was next aware
that he and I were in wheezing flight on the avenue.
Every few strides he looked over his shoulder. At length
he stopped and bent, hands on knees, butt butting
a parking meter. My heart pounded with violence
love did not know; were I not immortal
I would have been dead.

The Nubian came after us, penetrating my vaporous cover
like an arrow. How could he shake my hex? Did
daily narcotics give him powers beyond ordinary?

Myron's knees failed me; I could not flee. I interposed
my gelatinous bulk between swooning Stanley and
our muscular assailant. How would I safeguard Stanley
without committing an act so godly that
it would expose my magnificence? The Nubian
was closing too quickly; I could not think.

As if by divine hand, between the Nubian and us appeared
a woman with skin of burnished ebony, raven eyes,
teeth of perfect ivory, hair like rivers of darkened corn,
body magnificent in abundance and proportion. The Nubian
had to choose: vengeance against us, or pursuit of her.
He was soon at her shoulder, speaking of the fine evening.

Stanley did not know the Nubian never felt his blow.
By his flight, his offer of tribute, Stanley revealed himself
as inclined to combat as a moneyed hare. Still,
he fought for me though he was free to flee a conflict
I incited. Achilles would have sulked in his tent and
left me to my fate; great god Ares might have struck, but only
if he were in the mood for mayhem.

Could I help but love thin-limbed Stanley for his act?
Greater now was my desire to bring him blessings
of Catskill. But how much longer until I would learn
how to bestow them?

Black magic

Stanley's wind returned slow as bread rises. Then he said, "Are you insane? Nubus! You're lucky he didn't kill you."

I said, "True, every word of it. Can you think of a better explanation?"

He said, "I didn't realize you have such a problem with blacks."

I said, "I don't. So far they're more interesting than tans."

He said, "So far? Don't even tell me what that means."

The pedestrian volume was great. Two women before us
wore skirts so distended by nates that I feared
their imminent unseaming – an erotic artifice unknown
to the draped beauties of Catskill. Their legs were wrapped
in black netting, as if they had been free-swimming
until hoisted by fishermen onto dry earth. And the shoes:
surpassingly high-heeled, far separating them from
unnerving thoughts of the underworld.

Passing cars slowed, windows open, so young Nubian men
could spatter them with carnal suggestions. Then
appeared a car tipped sharply toward the front.
When it pulled to the curb a man with light brown skin
thrust out his head and said this: Ssss. The car
pulled away with wheels asqueal.

Stanley of the reviving flesh tone said, "I never understood why guys do that. It's not like it's going to get them anywhere."

I asked if he would like me to explain. He said, "Not if it has to do with Nubus."

I laughed. "Nubus? Foolish fellow. This is the work
of the beautiful and elusive goddess of cats, Nap. A denizen
of the deep woodland, she shows herself at forest's edge
only once a year, when her thoughts turn to love. There,
suitors from all lands wait to plead for her favor.
Once a temerarious aspirant from a distant island
violated her domain and came upon her during
secret glossal rites.

"Nap might easily have slaughtered him, but preferred to play.
She clawed off his sleeves – and condemned his descendants
to forever wear sleeveless underwear for all to see.
She slashed his lying mouth; his scions must wear
thin moustaches as stripes of dishonor. Whenever
they attempt to woo, no words issue; instead
they say only: Ssss – lest they forget their forebear's
feline desecration."

Stanley short sleeves stared at me. He said, "It's like you're talking in tongues. Did you ever see the movie *Escape from New York*? An evil scientist implants a device in a guy's head and sets it to explode if he doesn't get out of the city in time. Myron, I believe that you are that very man. I believe your head is about to explode."

I said, "Do you have a better explanation?"

We passed a lot vacant save for concrete debris
and rusting iron. Then came to view a carefully laid
circle of bottles filled with colored water, each
supporting a lit candle. The air was suddenly foul;
Stanley's nose sensed it soon as mine. Black silk bags
hung from trees above. We were alone; other mortals
avoided the area.

Stanley pointed up and said, "What in the world are those?"

Immediately upon question's end, a large bag fell atop him,
dropping him stunned to the cracked pavement.
In the bag I found a chicken, large and lifeless.
I could not ignore this incident, rare even by earthly standards.
Stanley's injuries were superficial; I made another
departure from him.

Before the next urine-soaked tenement was an alley
leading to a low building painted with geometric decorations –
primitive by Attic standards, but coruscating with passion.
A brightly illumined cross mounted on an inner wall
was circled by plastic men with beards and halos
and beatific looks. But this was no church.

All inside were pure-blooded descendants of Nubus.
I considered mutating into that form; but the pain
of my last transformation still lived with me. I appeared
at the door in current incarnation – equally objectionable,
I thought, to humans of all race.

An imposing mortal with great gray beard prevented
my intrusion. I looked unwaveringly into his eyes;
after lengthy silent communion, he ushered me

into the room. The holy man was the first of
this thick species to discern my divinity.

A rite was in progress. Prominent was an elaborate heart
drawn of white powder on the floor. Of course! Despite
fine clothes and genteel aspect they, like the Nubian,
were loving merchants in narcotics. Yet my godly nose
could detect none of it; rather I smelled flour. Nor
could I imagine the Nubian laying chickens, necks slit,
eyes slowly yellowing, atop the precious powder,
as these mortals had. Chickens were not offered at Olympus.
They had been, however, the fundament of Catskill.
These people, I realized, were altogether more godly
than the Nubian.

Through the far portal entered a woman, within a phalanx
of three men. All eyes turned to her; all talk ceased.
In erotic flame she was equal to the one who spared us
the wrath of the Nubian; but this woman trod the floor
with special resplendence.

Draped with gold and pearls, redolent of flowers,
she toured the room, enfolding the men, pressing
full-bodied against the most favored; and vouchsafing
limp fingers into palms of the women. She was offered
great bouquets and platters of dainty cakes.

Three drummers began a beat of magical pitch and rhythm;
there were no lamenting lyrics here. The woman chose
a young man nearly my equal in beauty to join her in dance.
The floor cleared: Terpsichore, muse of dance,
could not have choreographed more gracefully.

Moments later change seized the woman; her shoulders
rolled wildly, whirling her head as if her neck had no sinew;
her eyes lost focus; mortal spirit was abandoning the body,
human restraint yielding to something greater. Soon
she was pure, guileless femininity. I could not
decode the room's patois, except for her name,
whispered again and again: Erzulie. Who was she?

Myron and I concurred for the first time: we were her thralls;
she exceeded the sum of all women in Brooklyn. Yet
her innocence was forbidding; I did not know
that I could have her – certainly not as fat white man,
perhaps not even as perfect deity.

The room was hers; but power did not satisfy.
Her aspect again changed: the rapture, the transcendence,
seeped from her face. She began to weep. When her feet
ceased their magic motion, the drums halted. She pointed
to her partner and charged he did not love her;
he fled her wrath. To a cadence of her own sobs
she spoke of an engagement, years ago,
broken by a heartless fiancé.
"Life is pain!" she cried.

Men reached to comfort her; she slapped back their hands.
She went limp as if felled by bloody Ares' spear;
she was helped, unconscious, from the room.

Myron's heart pounded within me; others in the room
began to eat. Was this the end? Was love here so abrupt?

I needed inquire. I worked toward the priest; people parted
resistively as briars. Before I reached him, new drums
began a new beat: jarring, syncopated. The woman reappeared,
restored; her dance was erotic, but violent, wrenching.

Again she seemed to depart her form; a subjugating spirit
convulsed every muscle. Her neck was rigid; teeth locked;
knees met swaying bosom; fingernails drew blood from palms.
The voice, earlier high and flirtatious, was now raging,
primordial. I heard her new name: Erzulie Ga-Rouge.
Was she the same?

All in the room began to move; I included.
The swaying of our shoulders dispatched undulations
down our arms and spine; our feet had no choice
but to follow. As if guided by cosmic power,
we slowly formed a great serpent that worked
round the female presence. The drumming
pushed us to ever greater frenzy. For the first time
during my sojourn I felt the weight of earthbound Myron
lift from me.

Alas, happiness was dashed – not by drums, nor dancers
of Erzulie. It was the final figure on the sinuous line,
color jarring as blood on a virgin's gown, movements spastic as
a worm on a hook. It was Stanley short sleeves.

My departure from him was measured by mortals,
not gods; I had given him ample time to find me.
I could not allow him to absorb this rite; should it
distemper his undeclared white instincts, how would I know
his ambitions? I motioned to the priest; to his lead,
the teeming line turned. When we were before a door,
it flicked us through, as a snake would with its tail
shed dead skin.

I, scion of the goddess of love, reeled from the discovery
of a mortal complex and passionate as Mother
in a Brooklyn back alley. Could she exist
without Mother's acquiescence? Why here?
Did she not contravene the curse of Nubus?

Love on earth was more intricate by the hour;
and the hours were extending everlastingly before me.

The Krishna captivity

Back on the garbage-strewn street, Stanley flapped and said, "I had some good rhythm going there. Remember the hully-gully?"

Again we turned toward the avenue to seek transportation.
Before we signaled, a car pulled to the curb; brown lips
through a fissured window said, "I think very much you two
fine gentlemen should get into the cab. Thank you very much."

Stanley asked why; the man repeated his entreaty.
I could not read him: was he an agent bent on
leading us deeper into Brooklyn? But who would risk
Mother's wrath with so unprepossessing a messenger?

A few moments later we were touring down Flatbush Avenue.
My immense nates raised sharp springs through the worn seat;
oh, for the soft moss of Catskill!

The driver rotated between us and the windshield. He said,
"You guys are very lucky I am in this place. I am usually not
coming down to this place. It's no good. Today I am coming
anyway, not on purpose. In Brooklyn Heights I saw a guy
jumping up and down, very upset about something, so what
could I do? I could not leave him on the street jumping up and
down. I am thinking maybe he is going to give me a good tip
for coming to this place. But he gave me a dollar, one dollar.
People say, Mr Singh, you are too much caring of people. But
I cannot help myself. I was turning to go back when I saw you

well-dressed gentlemen and I thought to myself you are in the wrong place. Are you coming from far away? I will take you back, it will be OK. It is very dangerous in this part. Anything could happen to you – one, two, three. What are you doing here anyway? You look very troubled."

Stanley short sleeves read his license. He said, "Well, Mr Ramompollah, we didn't plan to be here. There was an accident on the subway."

The driver said, "They call me very much Mr Singh. You think that I am only a taxi driver. It is not so. I am a physician, all the way from India. If anything is going wrong you are very lucky that you have a physician in your taxi.

"It is not an easy time, no sir. I am arriving and saying I want to help out these people. I go to this department and they say I need a license. I ask where do I get this license, and they send me to a place with signs, many signs. One person gives me a form, one person gives me two forms, and I am sitting many hours filling out these forms, and they say, sorry Dr Singh, you have to do a residency. I am saying, there must be a mistake, I have cured thousands of people in India already. Ask them if I am a good physician, they will tell you. Here they are treating me like a small boy. In India you can fix this problem. You are taking many rupees and you're holding them in your hand and you're saying I want a license for doctor, and you're putting it on the table and pushing it closer, and then you are a doctor. – I mean other people are doing this. Not me, no sir. I am going to all the classes and they are calling me number one. – But in this country they are forcing me to start all over again, like a small child. No one wants me in their residency program, and I don't know why. Maybe they are afraid because I will make them look like silly people for trying to teach a doctor who has cured many patients already. This is very terrible that a man of many talents is not doing his work. But you are lucky. If you are choking I will be saving you."

Stanley short sleeves said, "Dr Singh, why a cab driver? Why not another profession?"

Dr Singh said, "Can I speak truthfully? When I am driving I am making good money. My family is not here and it makes me a very sad man. I want to bring them over. I want to bring over many of my people. We want to have our part of the city, where we can be together, like those kinds of people."

A blare from traffic corrected Dr Singh's errant navigation. He continued: "Look at those boys out here. Look at how they are sitting on the cars. What are they doing this way? They are always out here. I can't understand why they are not working. Strong boys. Healthy boys, they can lift up a sofa. In India everyone who is walking is working. I am working all the time. I am a very hard worker, you can be asking anyone, even my brother-in-law, and he will tell you – there goes Mr Singh again. Am I taking this welfare? No way. Who is working in these print shops all the time, who is selling the newspaper and the magazine and the cigarette? It is my people. We are working very hard."

Dr Singh pointed out the front and said, "You look this way. You are seeing the towers of the Brooklyn Bridge. Behind that you are seeing Manhattan. I dreamed of it since I was a small child. The first time I saw it, I can tell you, my face was very wet with tears, and I was not embarrassed, no sir. Soon I am driving you across the bridge, and I am saying that this is no place for

gentlemen of refinement and education. I am hoping I am
never going to be seeing you in this place again. Soon I hope I
am joining you on the other side."

Stanley short sleeves said, "I am hoping that you do."

Dr Singh turned forward; our backs felt his acceleration.
Stanley did not demur; why, I did not know.
Lights spangled great structures across the river.
Across their small fraction of sky, they were more than equal
to the Olympian firmament: denser, brighter, more colorful.
But the builders of the mighty skyscrapers, unlike herders
of the sheepy lea, did not understand that the truth of stars
is in the stories they tell. I saw no tales in this electronic sky:
lights went on, went off, randomly – uninspiring
to men's hearts, perhaps even dimming them
with purposelessness.

All the more the surprise when Stanley said, "You know what
this view always reminds me of? A long time ago, god, it must
be fifteen years now, I had to go to London on business, and
this is pretty much the same view on the way back from the
airport. I had just met Eileen. But as spectacular as the view is
all I could think about was seeing her again. That answered a lot
of questions."

I said, "How long did she take to dim?"

He smiled. "She has never dimmed. I guess you can't understand
that."

A horrid screech! We were cast against the front seat as
the car braked, concussion imminent. What would

ooze from my broken form: godly ichor, or mortal blood,
whose savage color — if it were mine — I vaguely feared?
The deliberation was mooted when the car halted
without impact.

Stanley short sleeves cried, "What happened? Did we have a
blow-out?"

Dr Singh said, "There is something I must be doing."
His voice was suddenly deeper, impassioned, as if
it had been seized by his heart and dragged into his chest.

Stanley asked what it was; could we help? Dr Singh
threw open the opposite door. A woman climbed in
beside him. He turned the taxi hard across the cursing traffic,
back toward where we had come. She was dark,
but no child of Krishna; nor had she trappings of harlotry.
How could he see her on the bleak approach
to the Brooklyn Bridge when my divine eyes had not?
I could not believe this was an assignation, given
Dr Singh's passion for rescuing us; unless she too
was in need of deliverance. But how would he know?
No word passed between them; yet there was a radiance
from the front seat.

Stanley short sleeves asked if she were joining us
on our trip. Dr Singh said, "I will be taking you home,
gentlemen. Look at this, I am turning off the meter. But I must
be going this way."

Stanley protested to leave the meter on, and convey us
to Manhattan; we had boarded first. Dr Singh,
brown knuckles whitening around the wheel, said, "You see,

this woman needs me. I am taking her right away, without stopping. I cannot explain it fully. I am asking you to be patient, and I will be taking you home too."

Stanley said, "I don't want to risk meeting up with that guy I punched out. Dr Singh, pull over."

Dr Singh's eyes were wed to the striped road. He said, "I am very disappointed that you are not understanding what I am doing. If we are stopping at a light, I will be letting you out. But I cannot stop otherwise."

He blew like an eyeless hurricane, furiously in one direction, then the opposite. Another mortal mind proved opaque
to my divine analysis. I wanted to comprehend;
I needed time. I called for Utilitas to halt us with red;
he did not heed me. The neighborhood regained
the cast of the Nubian's; Stanley short sleeves grew agitated.
He grasped Dr Singh's shoulders and said, "Damn it. Pull over right now or I'll call a cop."

Dr Singh said, "I am terribly much disappointed. If you cannot see the truth for yourself, you should be trusting a man who knows it is most important to be caring for women. But you must do what you must do. I am washing my hands of the whole thing."

Dr Singh swerved onto a side street. Neither he nor the woman looked back as we debarked. The cab's wheels squealed
before the report of slamming doors.

Honk if you love Aphrodite

The street was narrower, calmer than our previous stop;
yet nature had been equally suppressed. But for
an occasional ailanthus, rising frail through concrete cracks,
no one would know Brooklyn belongs to a green planet.

My divine eyes espied stickers on the chrome of parked cars.
Madness! Cagey Odysseus plowed his field with ass
yoked to ox, feigning insanity to elude
the bloody voyage to Troy; even he never stooped
to gluing words to beasts, as if they could read.

I read to Stanley short sleeves: " 'God is the answer.' "

He said, "That's very nice. But my question is: 'Where is the
subway stop?' "

I read: " 'Honk if you love Jesus.' "

Stanley short sleeves said, "What am I, a goose?"

I said, "Do you believe there is a god?"

He said, "Do you believe there is a good dark ale without a
bitter aftertaste?"

I said, "Do you know who Aphrodite is?"

He said, "I swore by her for ten years. I consider her one of my
dearest friends."

What blackness was this? I repeated my question,
he his answer. He said, "I don't know what I would have done
without her. My life would have been a lot less exciting, that's
for sure."

I cast a Myron's doubt at the notion of any excitement
in his life. Then rose a chance for a question
I never hoped to pose in mortal form:
"What exactly has Aphrodite done for you?"

He said, "Didn't she do a lot for you too? Or are you a Trojan
man?"

A Trojan? A man? Contumely!

He said, "Or maybe you're a rib devotee, or day-glo."

I demanded what he meant; he asked if Nubian combat
had emptied my senses. He said, "I'm talking about Aphrodite
rubbers. What do you think I'm talking about, the goddess of
love? I've never had the pleasure of her acquaintance."

I said, "Rubbers?"

He said, "Condoms. What's wrong with you?"

And so I learned that Mother's name, which
I had not heretofore crossed among mortals,
christens a gruesome rubber cloak
over the glorious rise only she can inspire.

My love for Stanley wilted in his godlessness. I muttered
for Hermes to show mercy and collect me; Stanley overheard
and replied that the Hermes brand was so thick
as to suppress sensation.

I let Stanley walk ahead of me. Then I corrected the sticker
to read: "Honk If You Love Aphrodite!"

If mortals survive the murderous age of monotheism,
they will need help in their return to truth and beauty
and passion. The errant road from Mother to Jesus
is certain to be retraced, should mortals be reawakened
to what once they knew of true love.

Curse of the foreskin

Stanley short sleeves diagnosed my lagging. He said, "Your blood sugar must be down. It's been too long since your last beer. Come on, I'll buy you something."

We found a small store savoring of coffees, aging fruit, sawdust. Wonderful live fragrances. He chose cellophaned chocolate cakes.

Once outside he said, "You're right, there is something supernatural about this evening. Two check-out women kept talking to each other in Spanish as if I didn't exist. Right through my head. No one could be that impolite, so I must be invisible, and only gods are invisible."

I told him to beware. He said, "Eat your Ding Dong."

The next mortals we encountered were as a separate breed. I seized initiative; else I feared I would spend my eternity pushing like Sisyphus toward Manhattan.

I asked one if he knew the subway entrance. His eyes were on the ground before him; my voice raised them, reluctantly. He looked to want to escape us; but he was my equal in girth, and crimped by a long black coat; should he reach any speed his topsail-like hat and mainsail beard would catch wind. He said, "Are you talking to me?"

I asked again. He said, "Why are you asking?"

I said, "So we can get on the subway."

He said, "Where are you going?"

I said, "Manhattan."

He said, "Where in Manhattan?"

I said, "If you can get us over the bridge, that would be good enough."

He said, "There are a lot of ways over the bridge. Tell me where you're going, and I'll tell you how you go."

Stanley short sleeves said, "The upper west side."

He shrugged. He said, "The west side. It's a big place. You have an address?"

I said, "Do you know where the subway stop is?"

He said, "Do I know where the subway stop is? I'm a fifty-five-year old man. I'm riding it since I'm six."

Stanley said, "It's a simple question."

He said, "What's so simple? You don't have an address and I'm supposed to figure this out?"

I said, "Sorry to be a bother."

He said, "No bother. Glad to help."

A mother, bursting with child and amidst her issue —
nine children, each asea in vesture — touched the man's sleeve.
She said diffidently, "Mendel, the gentlemen are lost. Perhaps
they are hungry too?"

She motioned to the Ding Dong in my hand. Mendel
raised both arms to the sky; he slapped his forehead. He said,
"May I own seven penthouse apartments and seven Cadillacs,
and each day go to a different specialist, and no one should
know what is wrong with me if I am ever so rude again. You
must come home with us for Shabbos dinner."

Stanley thanked him, but said the subway was our ambition.
Mendel said, "Have you eaten? You haven't had time, am I right
or am I wrong?"

Stanley said we had to get home. Mendel said there would be
plenty of time for that. Stanley said we could not impose
on their dinner.

Mendel replied, "Impose? As Hashem told us, 'Love ye therefore
the stranger; for ye were strangers in the land of Egypt.' "

I could not divine Stanley's thinking. Was he objecting
to Mendel's offer of another delay; or calculating
more time would be expended parrying the invitation
than accepting? Was he indeed prepared to return home?
Where was the beat of this heart?

Mendel said, "Look, one thing at a time. We'll take care of the food, then the train. You can't dance at two weddings at the same time."

Stanley looked to me; I would not help. He said, "Well, maybe a cup of tea. If you're sure it isn't an imposition."

Mendel said, "An imposition? Feh! You are doing us the favor. As rabbi Ezra said, 'To share the fruit of your home is among the holiest of deeds.' "

Once inside the apartment, he introduced us to his wife, Tzippi, and the children: Shloimi, Channah, Leib, Moyra, Berryl, Shmuel, Gittel, Fagey, and the baby, whose ambition was certain to be cantorial.

Nothing in the overstuffed living room hinted at the majesty of the dining room: crisp linen shrouded the long table; china and cutlery gleamed with light from a crystal chandelier; candelabrum blazed from a thousand buffs. Myriad scents sharpened as young women brought in gigantic platters. Surely this was their altar.

We were twelve at the table; there was food for ten times the number. Stanley asked if more guests were expected; Mendel laughed. He said, "Don't worry, there will be enough for you."

There would be no quick escape from this rite.
With eyes closed and scarf draped over her head, Tzippi lit the candle; light warmed her ripe belly. She intoned in a language her trachea resented to the top.
Mendel later explained the King of the Universe

commanded them to kindle the Sabbath lights.
I could not imagine so modest, so useless, a request
from Zeus; he would insist the candle ignite a pyre,
perhaps even a city, a Troy.

Mendel crooned to the strength and honor of his wife;
strength she certainly had, from the size of her brood.
I longed to hear the lyrical voice of so amorous a woman,
but she did not sing.

Mendel cut two golden braided breads, and the table exploded
into action. Awestruck Stanley recoiled from the tumult
and nearly fell back from his chair. Mendel's hand steadied
him. Stanley said, "Really, a cup of tea would be fine."

Mendel said, "Sure, sure, you'll get your tea. But you can't insult
Tzippi. She has been cooking all day. This is gefilte fish. It's
made from pike or carp. Tzippi, my bride, what fish did you
use? Pike. A noble fish. May Hashem have given it a good life
before it came to our table. Then have some knaidle soup. You
know what is knaidle? Matzoh ball. Some knaidles go to the pit
of your kishkes like lead; Tzippi's are light like fairies' wings.
This is roast chicken. You know what is a chicken? If you
haven't eaten Tzippi's chicken you don't know what heaven on
earth is – crispy, juicy, plump, like a little baby's thighs. Almost
as good as my mother's, may she rest in peace. This is tzimmes,
which is stewed apples and prunes and carrots. Delicious. You
will never forget what a cholent is, a meal in one, dating back
to the time of the Second Temple. Geshmat! Brisket, onion,
beans, groats – it cooked all day. Very filling, but I see you've
got a lot of space to fill, my friend. Cherry Heering and Chivas,
only the best. Shmuel, pass the gefilte fish. Enjoy!"

Shmuel, as pale of skin and black of garb as his father,
though not yet so shaggy and portly, said, "What are you doing
out on Shabbos?"

Stanley explained our route while futilely attempting
to fend off Tzippi, who was piling his plate with food.
He said, "Really, just tea will do."

Tzippi said, "Two cultivated young men. I suppose you are
married?"

We responded. She asked if we had children;
I said I did – the Michael – though, since I did not know
if he was my sole one, I left off there. Stanley said he did not.
The question unduly annoyed him.

Mendel said, "Don't be so nosy. Let our friends eat in peace." A
few minutes later he said, "So what brings you this way?
Business?"

Tzippi interrupted. "Let them enjoy their meal. Don't prod."

Mendel said, "Prodding? I want them to know that if they feel
like talking, we'll listen. Is that prodding?"

I began to speak flatulently of life as lawyer, hoping Mendel
would interrupt; he did – it was not proper to so expatiate
on Shabbos. This rite of rest had enforced rules.
With pagan apologies I asked what else to avoid.

Mendel said, "Everything in the world has a soul, a place. If we don't respect that, the world loses meaning. This is Hashem's universe, not ours. That's what we remember on Shabbos. Do you understand what I am saying?"

Stanley said, "You mean like the way the breakup of the Soviet Union restored all of those countries to their proper identities."

Mendel said, "Chozzer countries! May they grow like onions, with their heads in the dirt and feet up in the air. We don't care about politics or so-called world affairs. The real world is in the Torah and the Talmud."

Stanley objected: while he agreed spirit is important,
only the hawser of government prevents men's lives
from being swept out into the savage seas.
I concurred with Mendel: kings have puny reach
beyond palace walls. Men – with aid and approbation
of the gods – determine their own fortunes; why else
run the mortal course?

At length Mendel, with grave countenance, turned to Stanley. He said, "I'll tell you about your outside world. We had a student sitting at our table and telling us about myths he was studying. Brooklyn College or some ridiculous place. He thought Hashem's words are myths, like the others. He told us about this meshuggenah Trojan war – maybe you heard about it? – which was fought over a woman, of all things. So these Greeks were ready to get into their boats and all go get killed, and they were worried about the weather. What did they do? They decided to sacrifice the king's daughter to the sea god. Can you imagine? People who invented mathematics and made all these beautiful buildings thought there was a sea god? So the

king gets up on the rock in front of the whole country and gets
ready to kill her."

Shmuel said, "Isn't that like when Abraham went to sacrifice
Isaac?"

Mendel exploded: "Do we have a sea god? An air god? A
schmutz god? Another excuse to go cutting someone's neck.
Their favorite hobby, mamzer goyim! If it was really for a god,
why do it in front of everybody? There is only one god, blessed
be he. When Abraham, may god rest his soul, went up to the
mountain with Isaac, he faced Hashem alone. Not the whole
peanut gallery."

I asked about Hashem's instructions in love; I wondered
if they harmonized with Mother's. Tzippi blushed
and turned away. Mendel, with arms spread like stubby wings,
said, "Look at my beautiful family, all of them. Could this be
possible if Hashem did not instruct us to love, to be fruitful
and multiply?"

What drew this obese hirsute man to his peruked wife,
or rather, her to him, with such time-honored regularity?
In them could lie the answer to love on earth, and thus,
perhaps, to Stanley. Alas, as mortal I could not inquire.

As immortal I consume no food; as immense Myron,
I was being taxed. Desserts came, coffee, cordials.
Our hosts' joviality did not wane. I nodded
to Stanley short sleeves; we should depart. I offered thanks.

Tzippi said, "You just ate and you're running off? You didn't
like it?"

I assured her it was wonderful; she was not mollified.
Mendel demanded to know our plans. He said, "So go in the
morning. What's the rush? The upper west side isn't going
anywhere."

We said we had wives waiting. Mendel said, "They'll be happy
you stayed the night where it's safe and didn't come home at
some crazy hour. Believe me. I know."

Stanley short sleeves protested; with persistent sophistry
Mendel defeated him at each turn. Stanley sat back
into his chair. I was maddened. Why was it so easy
to deflect him from his wife's bed?

Mendel said to Moyra, "Make a song for our guests."

Moyra stood, hands grasping the skirt of her oversized tunic,
neck stretched like an ibis. She sang a song; we clapped,
Mendel demanded another. And another, and
the evening grew ever later.

Drink, food, and above all, talk were glazing Stanley.
The push had to be mine; else we would end up
like Odysseus. Had not his years with Calypso,
and then Circe, begun with one meal?

I told Mendel that, flattered as we were, we could not stay.
A night without my wife beside me was unendurable.
I too praised my wife as he had earlier sung to his:
my strength came from her.

At length he allowed me to reach the door.
I thanked him and clasped his hand; he had much augmented
my mortal understanding. He handed me a brown paper bag.
He said, "Just an apple so you shouldn't get hungry on the
way."

I extended my hand to Tzippi. She recoiled from it,
from me. I was staggered by the affront!
Never in my endless life had a female refused me –
I, perfect son of the goddess of love, now by this
bloated udder of a woman! And but the touch of a hand!
I would strike her down like a swine at the slaughter!

So distracted was I that within a score of steps from
their building I stumbled and fell large-bodied to the ground.
Stanley stood over me, in irrepressible laughter; I let
cool mother earth still my rage.

Stanley said, "That was awfully nice of them. No one has ever
done anything like that for me before. And they seem so happy.
But I couldn't escape the feeling it was all kind of medieval.
Didn't you think so?"

Over Stanley's objections, I recounted
the curse of the foreskin:

More than two millennia past, the Hellenes, emissaries
of Olympus, brought civilization to the stiff-necked Hebrews:
it was refused. Those dusty tribesmen, consumed
by ancient fables, refused to kneel to golden Mother,
even to thunder-wielding Zeus himself, preferring
to retreat to their desert and fight for their one –
outnumbered, overworked – god. Each winter solstice

they celebrate a brief triumph over a greater culture: Hanukkah,
festival of lights in the temple. Where is the celebration
of its torching by the Romans soon after?

The ancient Greeks implored the Hebrews to exercise,
to bronze and oil their skin. Yet all in Mendel's home, and
in this neighborhood, are uncolored, unfit. Greeks gave them
togas of white, the color of beauty, of nobility, of cleanliness;
these Hebrews wrap themselves in shapeless black.

Zeus, god of thunder, condemned the Hebrews severely:
for perpetuity they will hack flesh from their own penises,
commemorating the physical perfection they scorned.
More: Zeus damned them to know greater
and more numerous truths than other mortals, and
to value learnedness above all; but
other mortals will despise and assail them for it.

Stanley short sleeves interrupted, "You mean, they were
condemned to make great lawyers."

I told him to review the wretched course of the tribe this
Hashem tends. Where is his muscle? Delicate nymph Calypso
kept wily Odysseus ten years; Hashem could not
hold Stanley and me one night. Tzippi and Mendel
would know no one in love but each other for all time.

For the Hebrews is reserved Zeus' cruelest delusion:
There is no Hashem.

The Tartarus local

Stanley short sleeves helped me from the calming earth,
his eyes halved by drink and mirth. I could not allow
Dionysus' potion to congeal Stanley and his intentions.
I said it was time to return home. He looked at his watch.
He said, "I didn't realize it was so late. But let's not rush and
ruin the meal. What did they call that dish, colon? Very unusual.
Very good."

He laughed. A man sated with food and spirits needs only
a woman to close his day. I was wrung with frustration.
The night was upon us like a lid on a pot; I feared
rosy-fingered Dawn would tip it any moment, to
the terminal disappointment of the goddess of love.
Sanity flew from me like a starling; I cried, "Mother!"

My deathless voice hurled Stanley short sleeves
against a parked car; his outline sketched a web
of fine cracks on the windshield. He looked at me as if
I were Hades, come to gather him. I longed to tell him
I am the force of all life, here to inflame, not extinguish.

He said, " 'Mother?' Do you mean that as an expletive, or were
you calling for your mother?"

I told him to forget it. He said, "Forget it? I've never heard such
passion from you."

I said Tzippi reminded me of Mother; I just realized.
Which would amuse Mother, or revolt her – even if
a likeness could be ascertained through wig and scarf,
and the mortal damage of nine children. It would equally
disgust Tzippi, being likened to a pagan deity,
though a perfect one.

I desired nothing but to set eyes on beautiful pagan Mother
at once, even if in my old station. If I could not
read love on this scrambled planet, or generate it,
I would spend all time near the one who could –
the greatest of deities. Who would decline
such a lot?

Even my capitulation failed. At the corner,
the steel grating, which I had trusted so implicitly,
gave way beneath us. Stanley short sleeves and I
plunged into the domain of broody Uncle Hades
and his iron queen, Persephone.

*

Mother favors me above her other sons, as she should –
Priapus, the hideous dwarf, wields an eye-high member;
Hermaphroditus sports pink parts of both genders.
Mortal lore of this age says that Rhea, mother of earth,
has equal fervor – gravity – for all, no matter
their displacement.

Mortal lore is once more wrong: Rhea yanked me
toward her immense bosom with twice the force she drew
Stanley short sleeves. It was I who first penetrated
the second grating, fifteen feet below the first; I also broke
the third, beneath that, and the fourth. At last
I reached rock, pure planet. Stanley short sleeves
landed atop me.

I could not see sky through our passage; it had closed
above us – this drop was premeditated. Why would dark Hades
or Persephone challenge Mother, who could sentence them
to passionless eternity?

Stanley asked if I was unbroken; I said I had been, until
his impact. He was groping; he could not see.
I could; one cannot do work of love without eyes
that perceive in darkness.

Before me was a subway car filled with commuters;
some sat; most stood, one hand on strap, the other
with newspaper. I watched for many times the duration
at Khoni; the car did not move. I noticed only then
it sat not on rails, but, like me, on rock. How could it travel?

I left Stanley and approached. The silence inside the car
was wrong. I called in, to no response. I reached out
to strike the metal door. My hand passed through
with no noise. I walked through the wall. Inside
I read the tale on a ten cent paper – stranded
during a transit strike a generation ago, this car
had been forgotten. Its inhabitants were dead; their souls
inhabited these shades – vaporous humanlike forms
with unearthly patience. This train, once an IND express,
had become the Tartarus local.

One of many obese men, I drew no reaction.
With Stanley incapacitated by dark, I could reclaim
my perfect Catskillian form – drawing first air
after five minutes beneath Poseidon's choking sea
could feel no more restorative. Still no one reacted.
Might the dead be immune to my power? What,
if not love, did they spend eternity contemplating?

I approached a beauty, legs lithe as young aspens
and hair a moonlit cascade. She absorbed my image
with blank eyes; at least Tzippi had turned her back.
My anger at her, and my passion, exploded –
I would have her! I grasped at her; she sifted
through my arms as if crafted of morning fog.

Her arms passed through me, and her right leg, when
I felt her against my chest. It was no protest of passion,
as mortal virgins rightly raise against ravenous immortals.
This was indifferent contact.

She was soon beyond, save for two points
stuck softly against me. Of her form, only these

was I able to grasp: they were gelatinous bags. I had seen
enough of the sunburnt earth to guess what they were:
implantations to distend her bosom, to make her a totem –
as if femininity were a matter of dilation. What male
would be inflamed by prurient grasp of dead sacks?

Where in the modern world are the furtive looks,
the artful gestures – even the artless gestures? Now mortals
weigh enough for two, women are reconstructed, and still
men will not return home to them. Had Mother arranged
this discovery that I might appreciate the full onerousness
of her duties? If rather she had arranged that I learn
how to discharge them and win her!

The quaggy orbs were not for Stanley short sleeves to see.
I reembedded them in the chest of the woman –
turned hag in my sight. I resumed my repulsive form
and led Stanley down the tunnel.

Shades – mortals who had departed the sunny earth
for the kingdom of brooding Hades – were as thick here
as the live in Khoni. Like subway riders, they avoided
our eyes, pretending – likely preferring – we did not exist.
They looked to suffer from terrible hunger. I offered
to slice a heifer's neck and let them drink of the black blood,
as had, gratefully, the shades of Achilles, Agamemnon, Teiresias.
One shade, in electric blue suit of woven plastic,
pants legs ballooned like cypress trees,
asked instead for Kool-Aid.

Stanley could now discern the vaporous forms, but
did not comprehend their significance. Upon encountering
a gamy shade in white shorts and shirt he said,
"Bruce? Bruce Link? Is that you?"

The shade would not reply. I suggested Stanley offer
a Ding Dong. The shade ate hungrily. Stanley
repeated his name.

The shade said, "Hello, Stanley. Why have you forsaken the
Brooklyn smog for the land of the dead?"

Stanley said, "Dead? You've never been the liveliest guy, but I
wouldn't say you're quite dead."

Stanley thought he had been clever. Bruce said, "Punch me in
the stomach as hard as you can. Go ahead."

Stanley said he was too old for locker-room challenge.
Bruce persisted; Stanley's blow passed straight through.
He turned pale as his dead friend.

Bruce said, "I was playing racketball with Sid Rosius.
Remember him? I took three of four, and he insisted on a fifth
game. Then blam! Heart attack. Right on the court. I didn't
even get a chance to shower and change before the ferryman
came. I smelled so bad they made me stand at the back of the
boat."

Stanley stuttered but could find no words. Bruce drifted away
without touching the rocky ground. We continued down
the tunnel. Eons ago the volume of souls presented no problem
for Tartarus; now the shambling swarms overflowed it.

Several small, pale shades stood motionless; plaques
at their bases indicated they had died once but their souls
had been rejected, sent back to the sunlit earth
to preserve space. In exchange for their acquiescence in exile,
extraordinary undeserved fortunes had been granted them:

Al Sharpton stood like a caryatid, his crafted hair
supporting a beam; the far end rested on the tiara of
Princess Stephanie. In between stood Kathie Lee Gifford,
James Taylor, Maya Angelou, Ross Perot, Kevin Kostner,
David Letterman, Diane Sawyer, and the Trumps:
Ivana, Marla, and the Donald. Did they know
tidy queen Persephone had reserved endless miles
of deathless latrines for them to swab upon their returns?

Stanley stopped abruptly. He pointed to a rise
in the grim terrain and cried, "I can't believe it! It's him.
It's Jesus Christ!"

A man was affixed to a cross. But it was not right. I said, "In a
business suit?"

We were fortunate for our living bulk; we could forge
through the myriad shades queued to fawn before him.
From close range I saw the man was not nailed to the cross;
rather it went up the back of his suit, holding him
like a scarecrow.

Stanley said, "Wait. I know that face. It's President Kennedy. My
god, not only did they shoot him, they crucified him. This has
to be a bad dream."

Why did the man command so much attention among
the younger shades? In this he seemed second
only to the great deities of the underworld.

Stanley short sleeves continued: "I can still remember hearing
about the shooting on a little transistor radio in school. If only
we had him for a while longer."

I wondered why JFK preferred the limb-stretching perch
on the cross, when he looked free to descend.
I found the answer in the rear: he can no more leave his cross
than a mortal can desert his own skeleton: he too is secured by
Hephaestus' golden shackles.

Two are inscribed with bloody Ares' name,
and two indictments:
one for losing PT 109 and its seamen while sunning, then
blazoning the act as a hero's;
the other for abandoning his warriors to slaughter
in the Bay of Pigs, and seeding far greater carnage in Viet Nam.

Athena's name graces one chain: this is for dishonor,
for playing on the longings of descendants of Nubus
while surreptitiously working to thwart them.

One shackle is labeled Clio, muse of history:
for riding to fame on a history of courage –
which, cravenly, he did not write.

The thickest chain of all wears Mother's name:
It is for the loveless exploitation of numberless women;
and the heartless humiliation of the graceful one
who was his wife.

Why did Stanley and the shades weep?
They should have rained the rocks of Tartarus
against his fixed form — and against each other
for having chosen him while on the teeming earth.
Could salt tears not be shed for a mortal of quality?

Stanley said, "I still can't decide if it was Oswald or a second
gunman on the grassy knoll."

A voice deep as the earth's core: *"It was a goof."*

No one could reach this pitch save resonant Hades.
He said, *"As a service I swept the surface of him. What gratitude
these mortals show; they made him a god. Though
a peacock dazzles, beneath its plumage struts
a naked chicken. When will they know?"*

Further down the gloomy tunnel, we passed several
small markers, engraved: white jazz; Black Panthers;
Betamax; Marxism; Dada; Pet Rock; Eight-track;
good ten-cent cigar.

Stanley halted again, profoundly, and pushed me aside. He cried,
"Mother, is that you?"

The elegant, gray-haired shade he addressed
would not respond; I suggested he offer the last
of the Ding Dongs. She said, "Is that the way you still eat?"

I handed her the apple Mendel had given me. She said, "Myron
knows about nutrition. Though I've got to say it looks as if
you've been getting your share since I saw you last."

Stanley embraced the maternal shade, only to have her
sift through his arms. He was chilled by her escape. He said,
"My god, you really are dead."

She said, "Had you forgotten?"

He said, "How can you say that? I was holding your hand when
you left us."

She said, "I suppose you were."

He cried, "Why are you angry with me? I've missed you terribly.
I think about you all the time."

She said, "Why didn't you think about me during the end of
my life? What did I do that you made me live like a hideous
marionette, hooked up to all those tubes. Didn't you care about
my feelings?"

Stanley put hand to chest in anguish. He said, "I wanted you to
live."

She said, "But I didn't."

Louis Pasteur's sacrifice of sheep – not for the glory
of Father Zeus, but for mortal intrusion into nature's
inner workings – so angered the ruler of the heavens
that he sent the curse of Medicare: it deprives humans
of a dignified bronze-bust exit from this life, instead
dangling them by a cord which longs to break; all the while
degrading them in financial battle with bureaucrats
indifferent to their plight.

She said, "You thought I couldn't hear anything in that bed? I heard every word, from you, and your sister, the doctors and nurses, and your brother-in-law, that dope. Why did you let him in the room? All he did was kept calling his office, as if anyone ever needed him. Every day, people standing around talking as if I was already dead."

He said, "The doctor said you couldn't understand anything."

She said, "The doctor. Do you see him anywhere around here? He's down below this level, with the other know-it-alls – the lawyers, the astrologers, the economists, all of them."

He said, "Let's not talk about that. How are you, Mother? Are you comfortable here?"

She said, "Look around. I thought my one-bedroom was crowded."

He said, "Is there anything I can do for you?"

She said, "Now he asks."

Stanley could not keep from trembling. He knelt before her. He said, "Please don't talk to me this way. I never thought I'd see you again. What can I do?"

Stanley lowered his head; at last the shade of his mother proffered compassion. She tried to soothe with a stroking hand, but it passed through him. She said, "You can't imagine how I've longed for this moment. Every day I stand by the dock waiting for the ferry. Not that I ever wanted you to be on it – but if you were, I wanted to see you right away. How distinguished you look. I want to hear everything. But, as we say in Tartarus, what bane has pinned you to this dark world so early in life?"

I assured her we were but visitors, still of living flesh.
She said, "If they are sending you back to the surface, talk to David Brenner about terms. No one got more with less than he did."

I said our sojourn must end. Stanley again asked
what he could do. She said their worlds did not intersect;
she could never again touch him, nor he her.
Much as her dark spirits had been raised by his visit,
she hoped it would be a long time before grim Hades
secured him here.

He said, "I love you, Mother."

She said, "And I love you, my son."

His short mortal memory failed him, and again
he tried to enwrap her in his arms. The ghosts of
watery tears streamed down her pale cheeks. She turned
to allow us to leave.

An instant later she turned back. She said, "How is Eileen? Is she well?"

He said, "Yes, she's excellent. I'd tell her you asked, but who would believe it?"

She said, "Do I have grandchildren?" He said no, not yet. She said, "Life doesn't go on forever."

He said, "I know."

She said, "I don't want to interfere, but I recommend that you don't wait."

Of all the provocations of the evening, this remark
elicited greatest discomfort. She said, "If you really want to do something for me, have a child. That's a lot less selfish than it sounds."

Stanley fumbled for an answer. She said, "The shades without children have their own level of Tartarus. There's a lot more room, but they are all out of their mind with loneliness – they have nothing to think about but themselves. That gets old during eternity. Now go. Bring Eileen some flowers and champagne. I feel better just thinking about it."

She gave him a loving push; her hands came through him.

Now I was certain why we had been brought
to the dark underworld. She was our oracle:
my task was surely to steer Stanley home to Eileen.

The bear, which wore condiments and concussions
of the evening, was no longer fit for presentation;
I left it in Tartarus. Should Stanley short sleeves still want it,
I was certain it would lie unclaimed upon his eventual return.

Young love

What stilled Stanley's conflict? His mother's words?
The hour? No matter. At my admonition Transitas
sped our train through Brooklyn and into Manhattan;
I would brook no further interference in this three-railed hole.
We transferred at 14th Street, then debarked at
the Times Square station for the final leg.

As we waited, Stanley pointed up at the metal grid;
rather, at a woman on street level atop it. Our angle was
the private view somber Hades has of all mortals
before he collects them. Yet the vantage also held glory:
golden Aphrodite imbues mortal underclothes –
which would otherwise merely sop sweat –
with erotic steam. My Myron eyes were aflame –
I chose instead to gaze at the gum-blackened platform.

I said, "Yeah, so? Haven't you ever seen panties before?"

He said, "This is probably what Marilyn Monroe looked like
from underneath when she did that picture. The one in the
white dress. Remember?"

I said, "For a few bucks any woman in this neighborhood
would show you anything you want to see."

He said, "This is much sexier. Look. She loves the sensation of
the wind up her dress, but she is modest too. Let's go see what
she looks like."

Again a delay! I said, "We have passed a hundred great-looking women tonight and you haven't looked at one. And now we're going to get out of the subway in the middle of the night because this one wants a little ventilation? You've got to be kidding."

He said, "I thought you would jump at the prospect. I told you age was catching up with you."

For the first time since the lead bottles toppled, I felt
Stanley's resolve; to deny him might be to endanger
my task, certain though I was of the ultimate wisdom
of the gray-haired oracle we had just heard.
I followed him up the stairs into the false colors
and sideways glances of Times Square.

There the woman stood, atop the subway grating, bent
to catch Aeolus' naughty upwind without exposing herself
to the uncertain night. Stanley was thrilled by
the sight of her; Myron too. I feared her, that
she had put aside her high heels and was taunting
ever-greedy Persephone.

Stanley said, "What a beautiful woman."

Attractive, yes, but not compelling. What gold
did he see in her?

His elbow struck my chest; it was not aggression,
but rather panic. He said, "Wait. I can't believe it."

He backed into a shallow doorway, and pulled me in beside. He said, "Take a good look at her."

His color was unnatural as the surrounding. I said, "Who is it?"

He insisted I look again. Myron might help here;
even if I could, I would not. He said, "Isn't that Eileen?"

I said the woman was far younger than his wife. He said, "I
know. But that's exactly what she looked like the day I met her.
She's even wearing the same clothes."

I said, "This is too much. You've seen her. Now let's get out of
here."

He said, "I can't. I'd spend the rest of my life wondering."

I could not restrain him without resorting to inhuman force,
which now I feared to employ. As he turned to her, I noticed
above us a row of modern Narcissuses in a garishly lit
second floor room, each lifting a huge barbell, each lost
in his own muscle-bound reflection. All that lacked
was proportion and beauty.

Stanley said, "Eileen? Is that you?"

Startled, she turned to him. She said, "Do I know you?"

He said, "It's Stanley."

She said, "Stanley who?"

He said, "Stanley your husband."

She said, "That's an original line."

He said, "Don't you recognize me?"

She said, "If you're offering to buy me a drink, I don't drink."

He said, "I know that. I've been living with you for fourteen years, married for eight."

She laughed. She said, "Fourteen years? That means we shacked up when I was in junior high school. You must have been quite the seducer, not to mention the felon."

He said, "I don't get this. You're my age. You're two months older. But now you look fifteen years younger. How did you do it?"

She said, "No offense, but if you're my age, the years have not been kind to you."

He said, "I mean it. Have you been to a plastic surgeon?"

She said, "Well, this has been charming."

He stepped atop the grating and took gentle hold of her upper arm. She eased free.

He said, "You really don't know me?"

She said, "You still haven't told me who you are, Stanley somebody or other."

He said, "And you don't think we're married?"

She said, "I get spacey about some things, but I don't think that would slip my mind."

He looked back at me in desperation. I shrugged.
He said, "What brings you to this part of town so late?"

She said, "A film festival at the Carnegie."

He said, "*The Seven Year Itch?*"

She asked if he too had seen it; he said no,
he had surmised from her pose. She spoke
of its exhilaration; he admitted to sharing it. Then,
save for the fluttering of her hem, silence took them.

At length he said, "I have to apologize. I am never this aggressive.
It just so happens that you are a dead ringer for my wife. Eileen.
Maiden name Costello. Only you're so much younger."

She said, "My name is Eileen Costello."

He said, "You weren't by any chance going to stop at the Chock Full O'Nuts on 72nd Street for raisin bread and cream cheese before you went home?"

She said, "At Bagel Barn. But it used to be a Chock Full O' Nuts. I hadn't decided whether or not to stop, but sometimes I do."

He said, "That's where I met you. Are you still living in that brownstone on the corner of 73rd and West End Avenue?"

She demanded if he were a stalker; he pressed hands
to heart – how could he express any intimate knowledge
without being suspect? How could he prove himself
husband? She said he would not want any woman,
wife or no, to display less suspicion of a stranger.

He said, "A stalker wouldn't know you have a favorite wedding
picture of your parents, and there is a glob of cake icing on
your mother's chin."

She said, "Where do I keep the album it's in?"

He said, "A trick question. It's not in an album. You have a little
table in your living room with a bunch of framed pictures. It's
there."

She demanded data an intruder could not know. He related
her family's long fascination with dachshunds, crowned
by her parents' current coprophagous pair: Daisy and Poppy.
She defended their habit as common.

He said, "So I'm right about the dogs."

She said, "Lots of people have dogs. But this is getting pretty
weird."

He described a painting, a street scene of Paris, filled
with bright-canopied indolence; her father presented it
on her eighteenth birthday. She returned a slow,
grudging nod.

He said, "One of the back legs on your bureau is broken. You
have it propped up."

She said, "With what?"

He said, "You know, I can't remember."

She said, "How could my husband forget something like that?"

He said, "Because I had it fixed when we got married."

She said, "That's a good answer. These are all good answers. I have to tell you, I don't know why I'm not screaming for the police. But they wouldn't believe this either."

He raised calming hands, and averred that even
should she invite him home, he could not stay the night.
She sputtered in indignation that no such invitation
was forthcoming. I was heartened; wily Odysseus
showed no such forbearance; thus I grasped to hope
that Stanley short sleeves' voyage would be –
perhaps even seem, if that were still possible –
twenty years shorter than his.

Stanley said, "I mean because of the bed. It's too small for me. It's your grandmother's, and she was tiny. Even your feet stick through the wire latticework. You would really rather have a bigger one, but it would feel like a betrayal. After all, Grandma Jenny did put you through Bryn Mawr."

She stepped back and said, "Enough. Who are you? I insist on knowing."

So distracted was Eileen Costello that her hands
abandoned her dress to Aeolus' wind, which lifted it
like lily petals around the stamen of her thighs.

When Stanley led her unto the weathered walk,
the garment dropped, as if to seal her fruits
for him alone. She rejoined her shoes.

It was simple to find a taxi in this favored land,
away from greedy Hades, away from dark Brooklyn.
Stanley said to me, "I'm going to stop at Eileen's place. We
have a lot to talk about. You can drop us off."

I feared their momentum once we boarded the car.
Eileen eased back against the seat; her lapped hands
were relaxed. This was wrong. I said, "You better come with
me, or you're going to get yourself into big trouble."

He said, "Thank you for convincing me that Tedious does not
have to rule every day of my life. I mean it."

It was time for a spell; I had many times seen Mother
direct them, with infallible result. Yet I had failed
to test my powers; I knew not what I could expect to cast
other than sweet desire, now the least desirable quantity.

Love had come to Stanley short sleeves; I could do
nothing to influence it. Had ever there been
more divine mismanagement? Mercy that Mother
was not here to see.

I remained in the taxi when they reached her building.
At the corner I debarked and returned to it. How could I
best enter her apartment unnoticed? The sole local fauna
were cockroaches; but love between them
is an unspeakable act, and I could not risk
being approached by one in ardor.

A vapor was safer; I chose pine, the scent of
a small paper tree in the taxi.

I seeped under the door. She was offering to offer
to tell him of her work, but supposed he already knew;
he did. She asked of his labors.

He said, "Do you mean now, or when I met you?"

She said, "Yes. Either."

He said, "I'm a management consultant."

She said, "Thank god. I thought you were going to say a tarot
salesman."

He said, "I liked it that you chose me even though there's not
much romance associated with my line of work."

She said, "Then why did I choose you? Or why will I choose
you?"

He said, "I didn't know. I won't know. But thank god you did,
or will. What do you think you're going to be doing in fifteen
years?"

She said, "That isn't a fair question. With most people it's
speculation; with you I guess it's true or false."

He said, "So it's not impossible that you might be married to
me."

She said, "Don't you think that question should wait for our first date?"

He said, "This is like trying to understand relativity – you know, the guy's twin flies off near the speed of light, and comes back younger."

She said, "Tell me again. What exactly are you younger than?"

He said, "Not me. You. You are my age, two months older, in fact. But now you are as young and alluring as you were the day I met you. Not that you don't remain alluring."

With the apprehension all seers report of their supplicants, she asked of her future: was it wrinkled and decrepit? On this one subject, the short-sleeved mortal was equal to any oracle – for fifteen years ahead. No, he assured her. Save for her hair, cut short for maintenance, and fine character lines in her face, she will remain much as is.

She said, "Character lines? That sounds bad. And I'm going to cut my hair? I can't believe it. It's a cliché."

He said, "Trust me, you're one of the few women who can compare with you."

She demanded to go dancing at once; it would lift her spirits, stave off her deterioration. Perhaps, she hoped, help preserve her hair at full span.

Stanley had not danced in years; nor did he share her belief in its liberating powers. He said, "Staying out way too late to gyrate in front of loud, bad music among sweaty people loses its appeal. What can I say?"

She said, "This doesn't sound good. What else have I missed out on with you?"

He said, "Nothing important."

She said, "You may not be the best judge of that."

He wanted no more than to wash in the glory
of beholding her anew after fifteen years. But
she anticipated fifteen years for that, and
demanded a more kinetic celebration.

He said, "I don't want to see places. I just want to see you."

She said, "See me on the dance floor. I'm pretty good."

He said, "I don't know what happens after tonight. If I don't have much time with you, I don't want to squander it deafened by a two-ton woofer."

She said, "Don't make me old."

He said, "You don't get old. You just get wiser and calmer. It's nice."

She said, "Look, Mr Stanley something-or-other, I admit that
I'm extremely attracted to you, and it usually takes me much
longer to get interested in a guy. But this me is raring to go out.
It's probably all this weird energy you're producing in me. If
you fell for me this way once, you're going to do it again.
Right?"

He said, "I would fall for you at any age."

She said, "Any age? What if I were older than you?"

He said, "I happen to know what you're like in fifteen years and
I like it a lot."

She wondered if love for them changes. He paused.
Beauty visited his plain visage. He said yes, it does.
After first meeting her, in his passionate youth, he
could not have believed it possible.

Stanley short sleeves fell silent. He took her hand;
she was glad to surrender it. He looked into her eyes
as if to seek a fundamental truth. Her expression
was bold, enticing; but I still could not read their souls.
The night was being decided without me; I was losing Stanley,
and I was losing Mother.

At length Eileen said, "Is something wrong?"

He stood up, pulled her up, and embraced her. He said, "I
cannot believe I'm saying this, but I have to go."

She said, "I can't believe it either!"

He said, "You are the sexiest woman I've ever known. But I feel like a company overstaffed with old men with green eyeshades, and you are a new, lean, mean, high-tech world-beater. I am probably better suited to my antiquated ways, and you deserve the sky."

She said, "I don't want you to go. But I don't think I am ready to give up the sky."

He said, "I wouldn't want you to. Still, I can't help hoping we will find a way to do business some day."

She kissed him. She said, "After tonight I don't know anything. But somehow it feels better this way."

Old love

Once ushered by Transitas home, Stanley stole inside
his apartment with sole-bending stealth, navigating by
scattered beams from Utilitas' lights outside. He began
to disrobe in the living room; I remained, in vaporous form,
little as I desired to witness his pallid flesh.

A voice from the black said, "Darling."

Startled Stanley caught an exiting foot in his pants and fell.
The woman rushed to him. She said, "Are you all right?
I didn't mean to scare you."

She lit the room. He said, "Sweetheart, you're still up?"

She said, "Of course. You know what tonight is."

He said, "Yes, I suppose I do."

She wondered why, then, so late a return; he demanded
his right to an annual reunion with his friends; she
did not dispute it.

He said, "I'm sorry; I didn't mean that. We had some amazing
trouble getting home. You wouldn't believe it."

She said, "I might."

He told her about felling the bottles to win the bear,
now, he realized, lost; about the cataclysm on the Cyclone;
about the Long Island seduction of Lennie;
about the subway car and its denizens from the deep;
about his compression by the wanton women;
about the Nubian, and Myron's dalliance with death;
about enchanting Erzulie and her dance of love;
about Dr Singh and his unfair turnabout;
about the stupefaction of the tzimmes;
about the legions of Tartarus.
He suggested that throughout I, true Myron,
had been queer as the rest. All he elided
was his encounter with the earlier her.

Her aspect betrayed neither belief nor disbelief –
only relief at his return. She kissed him, whispered love;
he replied in kind. They sat quietly, fingers knitted.

She said, "You must be exhausted."

He said, "A beer might be restorative."

She secured him one. He asked after her evening; it
was quiet and literary. Silence fell again; to the scion
of the goddess of love the inactivity was unaccountable.

She again left the room, his eyes with her. He knew
her mission: the longer her absence, the more foreboding
his smell. At last the rub of the evening –
his adamancy against coming home to this kind woman –
was about to declare.

Upon her return, Stanley looked not at her face
but at her hands; they palmed something
in practiced blackguard's grip.

She said, "We should have done this in the morning."

He said, "Maybe we can give nature another chance."

She said, "My love, nature has left us no choice."

He said, "What if we wait until the morning. Tomorrow
morning for sure."

She said, "It already is tomorrow morning."

Stanley, no longer short sleeved, but bare from waist up,
was exposed and vulnerable. He said, "Do you remember the
day we first met?"

She said, "Do I remember my name?"

He said, "Raisin loaf and cream cheese, right?"

She said, "Of course."

He said, "Did you ask me up to your apartment that night?"

She said, "I wanted to, but I knew that if I succumbed to your
charms then you might not have stuck around. A girl has to
make a fellow wait. Why?"

He said, "No reason."

She said, "I'm ready to succumb now."

She rose. Her robe fell to her feet; she looked
to have descended from an Attic frieze, so elegant and erotic
was her diaphanous gown. Stanley watched closely.
Her motions became a subtle mating dance; she drew
sleeves across his face. Still he was inert.
What ailed this mortal?

She asked that he take her; he replied he could not –
not yet. She suspected he worried about hurting her;
she did not mind. He said he knew this to be false.

She exposed her breasts, defiant of their years,
taut with expectation. She said, "Since I'm forcing it on you,
you're entitled to see the whole package."

He said, "A nice package it is."

She said, "Please, Stanley. Help me. I feel like a damned fool
standing here like this."

He plaintively wished he could. She begged not to
be obliged to act alone; even should he gore her it would
be preferable, that the goring was joint.
Admitting himself pathetic, he said he simply could not.

She said, "After all we've been through… Just look past this one
unpleasant moment. Think about coming in that door and
seeing a child raising his arms so you'll pick him up. Isn't it
worth it?"

She stroked Stanley's shoulder and revealed the other palm:
in it was a gleaming dagger, the more menacing
for an extraordinary fineness, which looked calculated
to defeat impermeable armor, via seams, between fibers.
He would not take it.

She pleaded: "Don't make me do this."

He looked away. She raised her gown and plunged
the needle hilt-deep into her own taut buttock; teeth
compacting her lips could not suppress a scream.
Upon evulsion, two crimson drops traced down
her milky skin.

Until that instant I was certain the potion was destined
for him – a Dionysian invigoration, as men have long required
between daily labor and bed! No, it was for her, though
her concupiscence glowed through her gown.
I was confounded.

If not a potion to inaugurate love, nor a temporary aid
to help celebrate it, what supplement would she dare
impose on Mother's perfect packet of passion?

The child! It had to be! She could not have obtruded
such a thought now, where it had no place,
unless she had longer purpose!
This needle carried no narcotic; it was
a synthetic humor to make a baby, to coax life
from a womb time and nature had stilled!
Mortal ambition had gone amok!

Stanley ran; I followed. On a bed he sat and buried
head in palms. Salt tears ran. At last I read
his passions: it was not outrage, such as welled in me.
No, it was rage at his cowardice. Most cowards
will not show this way. This one felt more –
love for her he was wronging. A man less loving
would have been less moved by failure.

At last I knew: though no hero, he was a lover,
worthy of my aid – he was a lover, lost without my aid.
My instincts, the night through, had been true.

Yet what of technique? I recalled wise Athena's presentation
of long-suffering Odysseus to patient Penelope:
I could bring Eileen to Stanley, refine her features,
sweeten her scent, firm her figure –
though there was little to improve. I could bring him
to her, broaden his shoulders, deepen his chest, thicken
his hair – though she was sure to be indifferent
to the change. But Athena had the advantage of war:
if I could retrieve Stanley after years apart,
passion would be simple to effect. Here I faced
overfamiliarity, calculation, technology – formidable,
all.

I poured sweet desire over the fallen pate of Stanley –
in no mean portion. He shuddered, but did not rise,
as if briny tears welded head to hands.

I did not measure my next dose, but deluged him;
he started like an infatuant of Erzulie. But he soon stalled,
wretched, ultimately unmoved. Odysseus alone
could string his mighty bow – it would take

more than might to affix the working strings to Stanley's heart.
Impotence so saturated the room – his at his task,
mine at mine – that through my new mortal pores
leaked an emotion unknown in Catskill: shame.

I returned to Eileen; she had rewrapped herself
and fallen to the couch, eyes fixed beyond
the wall before her. Run pigment stained her cheeks.
A dose of sweet desire would bring her to her husband;
but I could not withstand another rejection;
nor would I subject her to one.

Aurora's faint streamers were at last tinting the window jamb.
Reconstituted to my perfect form, I pressed
tapered hands to sculpted temples. Why was I here?
To aid my mortal charge. What did he desire above all?
To love his wife. His heart could not overcome
his body's revulsion at her medicinal demands;
nor could my spell.

But Stanley wanted more: that she feel loved,
that she have family. These I could do, I would do.
Is hearth not as dear to Aphrodite as bed?
Would this judgement not win her for me?

I effected the transformation into a likeness of
Stanley with none of the torture of that into
massive Myron – Stanley was more my proportion;
too, I had gained skill in this chameleon feat.

Eileen was surprised by my sleeveless return. She
wiped her cheeks, attempted to smile. I apologized
for my retreat, averred my readiness. She drew me

to her firm form, reassured me, swore it did not matter
since I was back. I wrapped her in my deathless arms
and laid her on the couch. We kissed; she was intoxicated
by my Catskillian scent without realizing; hers pleased me
like none I had encountered since my descent. Her hand
pressed my nape; her body burned through her gown;
her lips devoured. I entered her; the passion of her mortal form
was so great as to quicken my godliest feelings.

When I spent she did not release me, but clasped me
and whispered poetry of adoration. This time, she said,
we had done it, we would have a child. She could feel it.
This time it was magic.

And thus I experienced true love on this temporal earth.

Motherly love

Morpheus bore Eileen into slumber. Her husband
might later come to her and second my act, and think
my progeny his. No matter; I had done godly for him:
I reawakened love in his home and presented him
family, more remarkable than he could imagine.

I awaited fleet Hermes' advent and reflected: who
among the pantheon had debuted with greater skill
than I? My thoughts flew to the presentation
I would make. I could feel the goddess of love
considering me anew.

Strange feelings intruded; I looked again upon Eileen's
sleeping form, wrapped in her own content arms.
Was she so compelling? Her middle-age physiognomy
should not so discompose me. There was a
lure more powerful about. I soon realized:
it was scent.

I flared my godly nostrils and traversed her form.
The scent was not hers. It was the perfect perfume,
scent of scents. Aphrodite, goddess of love,
was nigh.

Mother had come! She risked her perfect beauty
on the smudgy earth to proffer herself. A mist
passed beneath the door; her divine form materialized,
as it once had from ocean foam.

I said, *"Nothing could soothe my earth-rasped eyes*
as do you, perfect Mother. But you need not
have journeyed. I was destined for your lair."

She said, *"My son, my emissary, I have come*
to hear what in my name you have wrought."

I recalled my boast in her perfumed chamber, that
I would not fail. I had made it good.

She demanded what exactly was made good.
I begged her not to encourage me to strut, much as
I felt my back stiffen and my tail rise. I asked
the deed speak for itself.

She said, *"What deed should I hear?"*

I said, *"Only on your insistence, goddess of love,*
I will recount how I restored an unfortunate mortal
to his home, identified the affliction of his heart,
and righted it."

She asked that I tell all.

I said, *"Recall, perfect Mother, it was your charge*
that my divine sensibilities select a mortal whom
you yourself might aid, and do with him as you
would. I did not facilely seek one exsanguinating
from a disappointed love. Rather, my choice carried
a strong but divided heart. He proved in great need
of my aid."

I described Stanley short sleeves; she allowed
he did seem in need; of his worth she was less certain.
I told her of the trials at Khoni; she disapproved my debt,
and thus hers, incurred to Squall and others.

I said I suspected Stanley's worth when he proved
indifferent to Connie and Sheila; Lennie was drawn into
the bar easy as a bee into a lily.

Mother stopped and pondered, in glorious pose.
Then she said, *"What caused you to favor bloodless Stanley
over one roiled by erotic opportunity? Is not he
more my child than Stanley?"*

I said I judged Lennie insincere, hungry for attention
of any brand – unworthy. Stanley claimed
an appointment with love. Mother bid me continue.

I told her of the twin terrors who drove us from the subway.
Mother wondered where his passion was then. I said
I still suspected time would make it incontrovertible to me.

I recounted the van crash; then our encounter with
the Nubian, who might have ended all, but for
the black beauty. Erzulie put love into Stanley's feet.
When Dr Singh conveyed us away, he would have
brought us here, save for the stranger with power
I could not divine.

The endless dinner, I told Mother, was difficult to escape;
less so the underworld, once the oracle had enforced
my conviction. Most formidable was the escape from her
whom Stanley took as his wife from the past. When
he left her for his coeval, I knew his love.

She said, *"But the deed. What was the deed that honors you?*
You describe yourself as mere companion."

As I hoped, she drew from me my true achievement: bridging
the rift between Stanley and Eileen with my own divine form.

She said, *"You lay with a mortal? Only once have I*
done so, and he was father of great Aeneas, founder of Rome —
even then it was not of free choice, but by trickery
of angry Father Zeus. You did so on your first night?"

Her displeasure seized my deathless heart. I said that
unto the tips of rosy dawn Stanley and Eileen had spoken
of family. I could not by spell grant their desire;
I had no choice but to employ body.

Golden Aphrodite said, *"Thus in my name you mounted*
a woman whose own husband would not."

I described the fearsome dagger, the blood it drew from her —
it was terror, not lack of love, that had driven Stanley off.

She said, *"Thus in the name of Aphrodite you sanctioned*
a woman be pierced not by her lover's passionate distension,
but by a cold metal tube; not into one of nature's
wondrous openings, but directly through flesh.
Nor was it congress, as it was executed by her alone.
Do I understand?"

I said, *"Golden Aphrodite, in this era, when women
first spawn at the age they were once put out
to die, this is how children are made. Are they
too not your concern?"*

She said, *"They are my concern, but they do not concern me.
If there is love, there will be children. Was this
cold steel needle filled with beauty and enchantment,
did it quicken the heart, surfeit the dreams? Only then
could it sanctify new life. Only then had you the right
to endorse it."*

I said, *"Tell me, laughter-loving goddess, was my summons
not to return Stanley to his wife, to bring them
to love again?"*

She said, *"You chose to prove your mettle in the fickle
flames of mortal love; you thought it would win me.
Understand: I care no more nor less for Stanley than
any other. Yet you praise him for rejecting my passion.
Should I be pleased?"*

Dread plunged through my sculpted chest. I said,
"Perfect Mother, did you say YOUR passion?"

She said, *"Of course it was my passion! All passion
is mine. Every step of this long night I was with you.
How else was I to judge you? I banished Lennie;
I saved you from the Nubian. When you were lost,
I led you to the oracle. Stanley's younger wife was I.
I was amazed you did not detect me."*

I said, *"Then you inflamed the twin titanesses to drive us
to the surface? And crashed the van? And led us
to Erzulie? And slowed us with cholent? And
turned Dr Singh about?"*

She said, *"Yes, all were my work."*

I wrenched my golden curls until pain rose
from my deathless scalp. I said, *"But why thwart
what you sent me to do?"*

She said, *"Had I allowed you easy navigation from Khoni here,
I would not know your aptitude with mortal love, which
is never simple nor direct."*

I said, *"Mother, your presence fires the human heart as I cannot.
However, I have observed what you cannot: after your departure,
embers of love can endure. These two mortals love,
I swear it. I was right to aid them."*

Golden Aphrodite smiled, gleaming as daybreak.
I had done it: I had won her favor by giving her
a tighter grasp of love on the murky earth. Suddenly
she evanesced.

All greater my surprise when next to appear was not
Uncle Hermes, to convey me to Catskill, but Mother again.
Her materialization from vapor was slow – feet, legs, belly,
chest, arms, neck, and finally, head – all, this time, of Eileen!

I could not imagine her intent; she said nothing.
I was discomposed by my desire for her, both as
mortal and immortal, and my fear of her. I said,

"You need not display your wiles. I am
first among your admirers."

She started for the bedroom. I took her arm; she pulled free,
her Olympian strength vastly greater than mine.

Her scent preceded her: wretched Stanley stood with eyes
of anticipation, color more than restored, respiration
deep and free. He embraced Mother's knees, pleading
for forgiveness. She needed not say a word. She let him
ease her into bed, just as I had her mortal double.

I said, *"You are going to breed with him? Hatch*
a mongrel brother to me? I cannot bear it. I lay with Eileen
to love, to provide family. I did as he himself wanted to do."

She said, *"And I am doing same for her."*

Stanley fixed avid lips to Mother's neck.
The heavens and earth were toppling.

I tried but could not pull him free of her; I would have
struck her, had I not feared the repercussion. Her
golden laughter, a taunting chorus of hell to me,
intoxicated Stanley. His hands were all about her like
fallen leaves in wind – this same man who had fled
her earthly twin in girlish tears.

He raised the gown of golden Aphrodite, exposing
to his view and mine the florid fountainhead of love
in this universe. I felt I would explode – so wrong was this.
I judged: Never. Never would he enter her, no matter her will.
I first realized: there are higher standards than her whim.

I held the syringe, the cold dagger, miniaturized by this
technology-mad age, which could part flesh more readily than
any Odysseus might have held. If Mother demanded zeal,
I would supply it. One quick plunge through Stanley's
sweaty back and I would fill his wan mortal heart
with air – thus ending him and this surpassing depravity.

I struck; Mother's hand caught my wrist an inch
short of penetration.

She rose and by strength of grip alone held me
against a wall. She said, *"Your deed has spoken –
it has condemned itself."*

My perfect head spun. After a night in pachydermatous disguise
I had lain with Eileen and expected return for it. Mother
had nearly coupled with Stanley and I would kill him for it.
She would equate the two. I knew her wrong.

I said, *"The truth, the love, lies in Stanley's heart.
In assuming his form, in lying with his wife, I felt it."*

She said, *"You have failed me by lowering love
to calculation. Love is lightning; it cannot be timed."*

It felt as if Lennie was numbing my lips. I said, *"Give me
one chance to show I am right."*

She said, *"Can you prove water is air?"*

I said, *"Have Stanley choose between you and Eileen.
Be fair – cast no spell upon him."*

She laughed and said, *"Between the mortal and me?*
I worried the soiled air would undo you."

Mother produced Eileen in the doorway. Stanley's head
reciprocated between the doubles like a vane in a gale.

Mother froze Eileen's features, lest they betray her confusion,
and thus her mortality. In unison Mother and Eileen said,
"Who do you prefer of us, darling? Only one is your wife."

Stanley protested this was impossible, absurd. But
the godly presence was strong in the room; he knew
to obey. He searched for clues between them;
there was none; Mother's likeness was perfect.
To my eyes Mother was wreathed in an amorous aura.
Stanley was blind to it; he was tuned to temporal frequencies.

He said, "May I ask a question?"

They nodded. He said, "If you were me, how would you
decide?"

Aphrodite erupted in laughter; the answer to her was
obvious as fur on bears. I knew this decided it,
so irresistible are her golden peals.

But circumspect Stanley asked the same of Eileen. She said, "I
am terribly confused. I can't even say this feels like a dream. It's
stranger than that. It must be even worse for you."

He said, "The worst part is our mating schedule. We can't let
anything interfere."

Eileen said, "We can't make love unless you're sure it's me. I couldn't live with that."

He said, "But you said it had to be tonight."

Mother said, "It does. Let's make our baby."

Eileen said, "Maybe she can go ahead. But I can't when you're not even sure who I am."

Mother said, "Don't let her confuse you. She'll delay and make you feel it's your fault."

Eileen began to cry; Mother stood beside her,
impossibly alluring, transcendently confident. Nothing
on the shocking earth could have prepared me
for what then happened: Stanley took Eileen
in his arms and kissed her. He said, "You are my wife."

Stanley's words penetrated Mother's mind like
wine into terra cotta – slowly and thoroughly; rejection
was absolutely novel for her. When her rage came,
it was profound. She melted into a pool of incandescent gold;
Stanley and Eileen staggered back. Mother reemerged
in full Olympian magnificence. She said to Stanley,
"Do you still choose her over me?"

Stanley's complexion regained its Tartarean shade. He said,
"Please don't kill us."

Mother said, *"Only if you lie will I kill you. Be careful:
I can read your thoughts."*

Stanley said, "God help me, what is going on? This has to be a nightmare; but you seem so real."

Mother said, *"No one is more real. Do you choose her or me? I demand to hear."*

He said, "She is my wife."

Mother's voice grew louder than I had ever before heard: *"Whom do you choose?"*

He looked carefully at them both. Then he tenderly kissed Eileen's hand.

He said to Mother, "If you really can read my thoughts you know that I think you are the most beautiful woman I've ever seen. Your beauty feels holy. I don't know why. But this is the woman I love. I choose to stay with her. I hope that does not make you kill me."

Fatherly love

Golden Aphrodite would rebound from her rebuff faster
than Dionysus from a surfeit of wine; she and I
would chortle in her perfumed lair. So I thought,
until through dawning downtown the laughter-loving goddess
threatened to pull my godly arm from its deathless socket.

I said, *"Perfect Mother, have I displeased you?"* She said nothing.
I said, *"When can I set out again to lighten your earthly burden?"*

She said, *"Never has a thumb weighted more heavily against
the universal scale of love. Into each mortal creature
I infuse the potential for passion. You chose Stanley, above all,
to aid – yet even in him you could not find it. If you would lie
with a mortal"* – she trembled with revulsion – *"let it be from lust,
not reasoning. That dishonors me above all."*

I stilled my mouth, but I knew her wrong. Stanley and Eileen
loved. Mother sent me to a changed world.

She led me to a room dank as the subway and nearly
as deep. She said, *"Now your second and final task on
the brown earth: observe your new charges."*

And so I came to see the fat hairy man in his saddle,
the faux-cruxified man with his zipped hood,
the yawning dominatrices who struck with the force
of feather fans – in this hell of false passion.

I walked the room in my perfect beauty; without
preposterous appurtenances I received no attention.

I said, *"Let us return to the sweet moss of Catskill. There
I can explain how I was true to you."*

It was then I felt cold cuffs close round my wrists.
I thought an eager mortal would make me his own,
bring me to the stage to flaunt his conquest. But I knew
from the strength the hands were immortal.

I turned to face Hephaestus, blacksmith of the gods,
with arms and chest of granite, horrid fire-blackened skin –
and lame sickly legs he cannot conceal. Husband
to golden Aphrodite, he cannot control her
amorous impulses, and hates all who remind him of them.
He crafted a marble malformed as he to link him and her
in the eyes of her mortal admirers. He failed; they revere the
Venus de Milo the more for its deficiency, and know not and
care not who was its sculptor.

Above all he hates me – my beauty proves I am not his issue.
Many times I have heard his desire to rid Catskill of me;
Mother has always laughed. I expect she will do so again.

I say to her, *"Your betrothed is with us."*

She says, *"I asked him here."*

I am surprised. He is her blot. I say,
"Because here he is equal among the ugly?"

She says, *"Today he is aiding me."*

Malodorous Hephaestus tugs the golden cuffs; they fit
like skin; surely the smith is greatest of artisans.
He says, *"How long I have waited for this day!"*

Uncle Hermes at last appears; a young man follows,
demanding the fleet god's alcoholic preferences, his
phone number. Uncle says to Mother, *"Let us depart."*

Golden chains lead from my cuffs through black holes
in the floor. Grimy Hephaestus says, *"They reach to the earth's core;
they can be rent only by me; and such shall never pass."*

This cannot happen! Not to the scion of the goddess of love!
I call to Mother. *"Hideous Hephaestus says you are leaving me behind."*

She says, *"Think rather that I am bestowing you with your domain.
Was that not your design?"*

I cry, *"You are my design!"*

She says, *"You think love need be solved.
When hearts quickened, you found ways to deny them."*

I say, *"I will convince you of the worth of my mission."*

She says, *"Convince me? That is not possible. I am the standard."*

I say, *"Take me back to Catskill. I will learn."*

She says, *"Love is an instinct. It cannot be learned."*

I say, *"But you're not going to leave me here!"*

She says, *"Watch the mortals don their costumes,*
perform rituals they have long planned. You can rule them
as I never could. Should love ever visit this room, people
would desert; only in privacy can they lose themselves
in each other. Here display is the thing."

I say, *"This imposture has nothing to do with Stanley and Eileen."*
Panic thuds in my thickening heart. I cannot again
argue my case; there is no time. I say,
"I love you, Mother! Do not desert me!
There is one brand of love: yours. This is but
a misunderstanding. Let us resolve it in Catskill."

She does not respond. I try to reach for her;
the golden chains hold my hands.

I cry, *"But your grandchild. How can you desert him?"*

She says, *"Your child I will nurture; he will not suffer*
for the disgrace of his father."

Tears run; they are my own, not mortal Myron's.
I say, *"How can you do this? Where is your love for me,*
your dearest son?"

She says, *"Before my love for you, or anyone, comes*
my love for love. I am Aphrodite."

Good night, love

Though Helios' rays do not penetrate the dungeon,
all know morning is upon earth. The crowd dwindles,
gaiety abates. Slaves are unharnessed by mistresses,
who are desperate to be in bed, alone. Loveless fluids
encrust once shiny black suits, now drab as those
who wear them.

Beside me descends the man from the cross. He removes
his hood and dons a suit like Stanley's before exiting
Club Hades. His mistress is long gone.

The Olympians too have departed. Soon I alone stand
in the club, fastened by the golden chains of Hephaestus.
Will Mother return to reclaim me, the perfect fruit
of her perfect womb?

The longer I reflect the more I worry that no, she will not.
Hereafter this will be my home. All know
Mother wields the vast powers of love. Today I have seen
she is also goddess of love's quickness and cruelty.

A blue-suited janitor removes glasses from the tables,
empties ashtrays, inverts chairs. He sweeps and mops
the floor. Before leaving he says, "I have to lock up now."

I tell him I'll have to stay the day. The keys to my chains
have left the building.

He says, "You're not the first. But the club doesn't open until ten tonight. You sure?"

I say I am afraid I am.

July 7

I got together with Lennie and Myron at Coney Island for our annual I'm-not-sure-what-it-is-anymore. Every year Lennie gets balder, Myron gets fatter. Their personalities are the same, only a little more so. It's a good thing I'm not aging.

You'd think that after all these years we could get home without incident. Not so. We got completely lost. I would write down all the things that happened, but I'm not sure what was real and what was delirium (too much drinking, and it was very warm). Or maybe Brooklyn is meant to remain a mystery.

I didn't get home until nearly morning, and Eileen was still up waiting for me. It was ovulation day. I knew it. She told me yesterday. I still don't understand exactly how they determine that. Temperature or mucus or something. The details do not help.

Making love on a schedule is not the most romantic thing. I'm lucky she's still so damn sexy. But whatever I try to think about, I can't get past the needle. That thing gives me the willies. It feels like I'm shoving a dagger into her. I actually ran out of the room this time, and she had to give herself the shot. Terrible. I don't know how other guys do it. Are they less squeamish than I am? Am I weak?

I should have gotten the shot out of the way in the morning. That would have given me the whole day to recover. Shooting her and then trying to make love right after – forget it. Everything goes limp, head to foot.

The worst thing is that when I fail to do it she thinks I'm avoiding having a baby. Wild horses couldn't get me away from her. I don't need a baby for that. I want a baby because

I want a baby with her. I really let us down.

Our futures can't be jeopardized by my fear of a five-second shot. Maybe if I took a different slant. Instead of a daily trial I should see it as a great adventure. I'm the loving husband, the humble warrior. I pit myself against the chaos that gods fling at us. The only one on my side is the goddess of love, and even she isn't all that reliable. I vanquish all enemies. I keep Eileen safe. I give her everything she needs. In these times, how many men do that?

I am a hero and a lover (though a small-time one). I have to say that to myself over and over. And then, maybe, I'll finally be able to do right by my sweetheart.